What others are saying about *FROSTY:*

"Gifted author Ellen Feld brings back the main characters from her acclaimed book *Blackjack* in this wonderful sequel. Not since the great stories of Marguerite Henry, C.W. Anderson and Walter Farley has an author so captured the romance and allure of horses for the teenage market. I loved every word!" – Hallie McEvoy, author of *Genuine Risk* and *Horse Show Judging for Beginners*

"Make room on your bookshelf for Ellen Feld's newest novel in the chronicles of Heather Richardson's life with her Morgan horses. A true delight for teenage readers, Feld brings us the sequel to her first novel, *Blackjack,* with this heartwarming story of Heather and her newest Morgan, Frosty, and their many adventures together. As well as being entertaining, Feld also teaches her young readers about horse healthcare and ownership. A sweet and charming story by this talented young adult author." - Christina Koliander, Managing Editor, *The Morgan Horse Magazine*

"In her second novel Ellen Feld continues to skillfully weave horse care and training information into the entertaining story of a young girl who loves Morgan Horses. Young readers are sure to keep turning the pages to read about Heather's adventures, while learning some of the finer points of horse ownership." – Jan Mansfield, Equestrian Journalist, Janus Communications Inc.

"This is one of the most engaging teenage horse books that this reviewer has read in quite a while. *Frosty* is a wonderful sequel to *Blackjack* and readers will be unable to put it down. Wondering whether Frosty and Heather will escape the woods of Vermont while at the same time trying to figure out what is wrong with Blackjack will keep readers captivated throughout this quick reading story." - Anthony P. Locorini, Editor, *NYHorse*

"Reading *Frosty* brought back a lot of fond memories. Not simply memories of being twelve years old again and mesmerized by one of my favorite books, but memories of what it was like to spend hours in the presence of good friends and good horses. The story, the characters and most important the horses are real and come alive in the pages of this enjoyable book." - Lisa Nyberg, who along with her partner Carol Hudson breed world champion Morgan Horses under the Treble's Morgan Manor prefix.

"Once again, author Ellen Feld combines education with entertainment in her delightful sequel, *Frosty*. Readers will be intrigued with Blackjack's mysterious illness. As strange symptoms appear, teamwork is needed between veterinarians to solve the perplexing problem. Clinical signs seem unrelated, yet come together in the end to help diagnose and heal a rare condition." – Ronald J. Emond, DVM, Candlewood Equine, LLC, Bridgewater, CT

Also by Ellen F. Feld:

BLACKJACK
ISBN 0-9709002-~~0-1~~
3-6

"Blackjack is a delightful book that will pull the heartstrings of any horse lover - it belongs in your Morgan library." – The American Morgan Horse Association

"Younger girls will be inspired...adult girls will remember back to when just being near a horse was all you needed to make your day." – Katherine Walcott, *Eventing USA*

"It is nice to read a junior novel that focuses on a teenager and a Morgan Horse. Ellen Feld has written a warm and rewarding horse story. This book would make a great present for a young rider and reader." – Hallie McEvoy, *Horsemen's Yankee Pedlar*

FROSTY

The Adventures of a Morgan Horse

Ellen F. Feld

Willow Bend Publishing
22A Mill Village Rd, S. Deerfield, MA 01373
www.willowbendpublishing.com

Library of Congress Catalog Card Number: 2003108243
ISBN: 0-9709002-2-8

Direct inquiries to:
Willow Bend Publishing
22A Mill Village Road
South Deerfield, MA 01373
www.willowbendpublishing.com

To my Mom
for all her love and encouragement
through the years.

ACKNOWLEDGMENTS

I would like to thank John Cowley, M.S., D.V.M. for his thorough review of this story as well as the wonderful care he gives to the real Frosty, Blackjack and Rusty. Thanks also to Janet N. Gordon, M.D. for her medical consultation and Michelle G. Hutchinson, D.M.D. for her invaluable assistance. Finally, I would like to thank Jeanne Mellin for the wonderful artwork she provided for this book.

CHAPTER ONE

A NEW FRIEND

The rain was letting up, but it was still a dismal day. There were thick, gray clouds filling the sky, refusing to let the sun break through. The ground had been turned into a big, sloppy ocean of mud from the early spring rain, and it was impossible to take a step without getting covered in brown muck.

Heather couldn't figure out why she had come to this auction. It always made her sad to watch all the nervous, unloved horses go up before the crowds as the auctioneer rattled off quick, insignificant facts about each one in an attempt to get somebody, anybody, to bid on them. Very rarely would she find a horse that looked healthy and trustworthy. Instead, what she usually saw were thin, scared animals, quivering with fear. They'd follow a handler up to the front and nervously pace back and forth until they were led away to their uncertain futures. Why did she come here? She already had a wonderful horse, her stunning black Morgan stallion whom she adored.

Blackjack was sixteen-year-old Heather's pride and joy. A purebred Morgan Horse, the stallion was registered as 'Gallant Image' but had been given the barn name of 'Blackjack' by

Heather. They had been through some difficult times together, but their trust and love for each other had always pulled them through. Together they had learned how to compete at horseshows and won many blue ribbons. But it was the quiet trail rides along meandering woodland paths that Heather enjoyed most. It was here that she could have her heart-to-heart talks with her beloved horse and sort out all the problems of the day. So why was she here looking at all the horses crammed into small paddocks?

"Did you find anything?" came a voice from behind.

"Huh? Oh, no, not yet," replied Heather as she turned around to face her friend, Laura. Laura was probably Heather's best friend. They had met when Laura came home from college to help care for her dad after his heart attack. Laura's dad, Chauncy, was the one who had taught Heather all about horses, how to care for and show them. He was also the original owner of Blackjack and had carefully guided the pair through some hard times. While Chauncy recuperated from his heart attack, Laura and Heather spent a lot of time together in the barn doing chores. They had quickly become friends as they discovered their mutual love of horses. Heather looked up to Laura and thought of her as the big sister that she had always wanted and took great pleasure in their similarities. Having gone to the same school, they loved to compare notes. They'd talk about which teachers they liked, those that they never wanted to see again as well as their favorite classes. Almost without exception, they would agree on every teacher and course. They both had bright blue eyes that seemed to sparkle all the time, even on the grayest of days. They also both preferred to dress in jeans and t-shirts, no matter what the occasion. However, in contrast to Heather's long brown hair, which was always worn in braids, Laura sported shoulder length blond hair. Regardless of the difference, many people thought that they were sisters, which delighted Heather.

"Did you find any good horses?" asked Heather.

"Nah, there's not much here. Do you want to leave?"

"No, not yet. Let's look around a little longer."

The two girls, both wearing rain slickers to keep out the weather, wandered around the grounds for another half an hour until a gentleman's voice announced over the loudspeaker, "Please take your seats everybody. The auction will start in just five minutes."

"Come on, that's our cue," said Laura. "Shall we stay and watch a little or go home?"

"Let's stay, just for a little while. Why don't you go to the arena and watch the start of the sale? I'm going to wander around for a few more minutes," replied Heather.

"Okay, see you in five minutes," said Laura as she turned and headed towards the arena where the sale was about to start.

Heather walked around the last two paddocks and was about to leave when she spotted a pretty little mare cowering in the corner of the last paddock. The horse couldn't have been more than 14.2 hands, and her hair was matted with mud and burrs. Her mane and tail were a mess too, with so many burrs entangling them that it was doubtful they could be removed without taking a good chunk of hair with them. Still, she was such an eye catching color that Heather moved in for a closer look. Underneath all the mud, Heather could see that the horse was a dark, almost black animal. Upon closer inspection, she saw that the mare was mostly a grayish color with a splattering of white hairs everywhere. The color was darkest near the tail and gradually lightened up towards the head. Looking at the muzzle, there was no black or white hair but only a soft layer of gray. Her mane, tail and forelock were all black and quite long and full. Perhaps the most striking feature that caught Heather's attention was that this horse had the biggest, softest eyes she had ever seen. On the rump of the little horse was a large white label with the number '18' written on it. Heather picked a clump of grass and cautiously approached the mare. Talking softly, the girl slowly put her hand between the metal rails and offered the horse some grass. The shy mare, seeing the grass, let hunger overtake her fear. She slowly walked to the rail, stopping just out of reach. Instead of coming close to the girl, the horse stretched out her neck and moved her lips in an attempt to grab the grass.

"There you go, tastes good, doesn't it?" asked Heather as the horse managed to get some of the luscious grass.

Seeing that another horse was being fed, a tall, lanky bay horse made it's way towards the two new friends. Flattening his ears against his neck, the muscular gelding quickly forced the little mare away as he grabbed at the leftover grass.

"Hey, that's not very nice!" scolded Heather as she pulled the treat away. "This isn't for you."

"Talking softly, the girl...offered the horse some grass. The shy mare, seeing the grass, let hunger overtake her fear. She slowly walked to the rail..."

The bold, ill-tempered gelding was certain that he could get some food from this new visitor. After all, everyone else who visited this paddock seemed happy to give him a treat. So sure was he that there would soon be some tasty morsel offered to him, that he thrust his nose through the rails of the paddock, and moved his lips in an effort to grab the grass. Unable to reach the treat, the horse then reached over the rails of the fence, stretched out his neck and once again moved his lips in an exaggerated eating motion.

"No, I'm not going to give you any. Now go away," demanded the girl. She turned her back to the horse and walked around to the other side of the enclosure.

"There you are," softly said Heather, as she walked towards the mare, being careful not to frighten the skittish horse. The pretty mare had wandered over to the far side of the paddock, away from all the other horses. As Heather approached, she again picked a clump of grass and slowly raised it to the level of the horse's face. The cute little mare slowly made her way to the fence, still cautious but having hunger overtake her fear once again. Unfortunately, the noise the grass made as it was pulled from the ground, although barely audible, was instantly picked up by the pushy gelding who was carefully watching this new visitor. He pricked his ears forward towards the sound and decided that he had another chance at a treat. Trotting over to Heather, he was pushing at the rails before the mare even had a chance to get the grass. Heather instantly pulled back, unwilling to give her treat to this intruder. Upset that the grass would not be his, the gelding showed his displeasure by flattening his ears back against his head and lashing out at the mare. First he nipped at her, then he swung his hind end around and kicked at her. The frightened mare quickly trotted away.

"What do you think of that one, Dad?"

Heather turned around to see a boy that was perhaps twelve, with dirty blond hair and a red and black-checkered flannel shirt and jeans. He was pointing at the gelding that had been giving Heather so many problems.

"That's the one I saw earlier today," replied the father, an older version of the boy.

"I've got a halter here, now which one did you want to look at?" came a third voice. An older gentleman, with black hair that looked like it hadn't been brushed in a very long time, dressed in jeans and a dirty brown t-shirt, approached the two potential customers.

"That one," anxiously answered the boy.

The auction employee climbed over the fence, approached the big gelding and haltered him. Eager for the attention, the horse willingly followed this person to the gate and out into the open where his new fans could look him over carefully. Heather watched the action from her end of the paddock but lost interest when she realized that this was her chance to gain the mare's confidence. She picked yet another juicy clump of grass and walked over to where the horse was now standing.

"Come on, let's try this one more time," encouraged Heather.

The horse looked at the girl for a minute, trying to decide if the grass was worth the effort. Slowly, cautiously, the mare took the few steps necessary to reach the fence.

"There you go," said Heather, as she fed the horse.

Within seconds, the grass was gone and the mare was looking for more. This time, Heather picked several large clumps of grass and offered them to the horse. Without the bossy gelding around to chase her away, the mare forgot her fear and eagerly ate the snack. Once again, the grass was eaten in an instant. Enjoying this treat, the young horse softly nuzzled Heather on her neck, begging for more.

"Oh, you're such a sweet horse!" encouraged Heather. She turned around and found more grass to feed to the horse. Returning with a third large bunch of grass, Heather fed it to the mare with one hand while she reached out with her other hand to pet the horse. Finishing the grass, the mare stood quietly while Heather stroked her neck.

"You like that, don't you?" asked Heather. "I bet you haven't had much attention in a long time. I wonder why? Why would anyone want to sell you? You're so sweet and pretty, and you don't look like you're very old. How did you end up here?"

As Heather talked, the mare continued to stand perfectly still. The horse gazed at the girl, her soft brown eyes looking so sad. It was this look that just melted Heather's heart, and that's when the girl realized that this horse had to come home with her.

CHAPTER TWO

THE AUCTION

"What??? Are you crazy???!!!" exclaimed Laura when Heather explained to her what she planned to do. "You can't buy a horse!"

"Why not?" asked Heather. "There are plenty of extra stalls at your dad's barn, and he said he wouldn't mind having another horse around."

If there was one thing that Laura knew about her friend, it was that once she made up her mind to do something, it was as good as done. Heather might not have all the details worked out, but if she said she was going to buy a horse, there was no doubt that there would be an extra mouth to feed pretty soon.

"What kind of horse is it?" inquired Laura, deciding that it was best not to try to talk Heather out of this.

"She looks like a Morgan except that she's gray. I've never heard of gray Morgans so maybe she's a cross between a Morgan and something else. I'd guess she's about four years old, very pretty, a bit shy but she has a very kind eye. I think that with a little love, she'd be a great horse. Besides, wouldn't it be nice if Rusty could have a friend to play with? I think he's kind of lonely."

"Yeah, I suppose Rusty would be happier if he had a companion to go out in the field with," replied Laura. With a ten-stall barn and only two horses currently living in it, the farm did seem a bit quiet. When she left for college the previous year, Gallant Morgan Farm had been a vibrant, prosperous farm. There were four broodmares, several young horses that were for sale, as well as Rusty, the older, retired show horse and Blackjack, the herd sire. But when Laura's dad had his heart attack, the decision had been made to sell all the horses, with the exception of Rusty. Rusty was an older gelding who had won many ribbons for both Chauncy and his children through the years. It was felt that keeping this special horse might help Chauncy recover by giving him something to look forward to. He certainly loved taking the gelding for long drives down the dirt road where they lived. But all the other horses were sold, including Blackjack. Determined not to be parted with her beloved horse, Heather had managed to keep track of Blackjack, and when the time came, bought him through an auction, much like the one they were attending today. It was this same determination that Laura saw on Heather's face. What made an auction horse so special to Heather?

"I don't understand," continued Laura. "Why do you want this horse? You know nothing about her. Okay, so she's cute. She's probably a grade horse too. I've heard of gray Morgans but they are so rare that I doubt anybody would sell one. So she's got to be either a grade or another breed. And don't forget, if she's here at this auction, then there must be a reason. Why would somebody get rid of her if she's so nice?"

"I don't know," answered Heather. "All I know is that there's something about her, something special."

"What about her gaits? How does she move? Does she have good action or does she stumble or maybe limp?"

"I don't know," admitted Heather again. "I couldn't get a good look at her movement. I watched her walk around a bit and she looked okay. But the one time she trotted, this other horse was in the way, so I couldn't see her very well."

"Okay, so we don't know how she moves. That's not good. And what about paying for her? I know your dad said that you could get another horse, but how much did he say you could spend?"

"Dad said it was okay to spend up to $900. Do you think she'll go for that much?" asked Heather.

"Maybe," replied Laura. "It depends on how eager people are to bid. Come on, we might as well go find some good seats."

Heather and Laura walked over to where the seats were. Cheap, metal, folding chairs, many of which appeared to have been purchased in the last century, lined the front of the arena. The two girls carefully made their way through the narrow aisle and found two seats in the second row. As Heather sat down, her chair shifted slightly and she thought that it would tip over.

"Whoops!" she blurted out as she adjusted her weight and grabbed at the chair with her hands. The chair once again shifted under her weight, made a creaking sound and then settled into the dirt of the arena floor. Heather looked around rather sheepishly, hoping that nobody saw her awkward fight with the chair.

The auction had started about fifteen minutes before Heather and Laura sat down and already the auctioneer was selling off the third horse. Although the arena was crowded, it didn't seem like a lot of people were bidding. 'That's good,' thought Heather. Maybe there was a chance that she could buy the mare. Unfortunately, by the time the fifth horse entered the ring, people were getting into the excitement and beginning to bid. Up and up the prices for each horse went until lot twelve, an absolutely stunning dark bay Quarter Horse, was led into the arena.

"Here we have 'Casey's Treat', an eight-year-old Quarter Horse gelding that has done it all. He's the one you want folks!" exclaimed the auctioneer, a slightly rotund gentleman wearing blue jeans, a denim jacket and cowboy hat. "This handy horse has won in the western and english rings but has really proven his mettle in the reining pen. If you're looking for a good reining horse that can score consistently high in the show pen, than start bidding! Now who will give me $5000? Do I hear $5000?"

"Here!" hollered one of the auction workers as he pointed to a woman in the fourth row. The two friends turned to see just who was bidding so much. A middle-aged woman, perhaps around forty-five, dressed as though she belonged at a fancy party rather than a horse sale, was smiling. The horse was led up and down the aisleway in front of the crowd, and when the bidding momentarily stopped, the auctioneer had one of the handlers quickly saddle and bridle the horse. Another helper, dressed in riding boots and jeans, climbed aboard the magnificent animal and, as the bidding once again began to jump higher, asked the horse to spin. Instantly, the horse effortlessly spun in place, making four quick circles. As he did so, his long mane and the ends of the reins both flew out away from him. Then he stopped, and just as effortlessly, spun four times in the opposite direction.

"That's really neat!" shouted a young boy sitting in the front row.

Immediately after spinning, the horse started cantering and, within the tight confines of the auction space, was able to complete two small circles before he was asked to stop. The elegant animal stopped so fast that he left marks in the dirt where his back feet had dug into the ground. Standing still for just an instant, the horse then swiftly backed up, perfectly straight for at least ten feet.

This latest action really got the bidding going and Heather and Laura continued to watch as the amount quickly reached $8000.

"Wow! Do you believe that?" asked Laura when the sale closed at $8250.

"I sure hope the mare I like isn't a reining horse!" laughed Heather, knowing that such high prices were well out of her range. "Dad would kill me!"

"Nah, he'd just make you sleep in the barn with the horses. But then you'd probably like that, wouldn't you?" teased Laura.

The auction continued, and while some horses went for a lot of money, most sold rather inexpensively. The majority of the horses at this sale, the scared, thin, trembling ones, didn't warrant a second look from most people. When lot seventeen came in, Heather recognized the annoying gelding that had tried to steal the grass from her.

"Here is a nice, child-safe riding horse for some lucky bidder. My form says that the horse is nineteen and has been used by a summer camp for the last three years. Who'll start at $1500?"

The audience was silent.

"Do I hear $1500?" bellowed the auctioneer.

Again, silence.

"How about $1200? Do I have $1200?"

More silence.

"Come on folks, this is a nice horse. Okay, let's have $800. Who will start the bidding at $800?"

"$500!" hollered somebody from the back of the ring. Heather turned to see the father of the young boy who had looked at the gelding earlier. Next to the man was his son, with a somewhat nervous expression upon his face. He obviously wanted this horse and didn't want anybody else to bid.

"I have $500. Do I hear $600? $600 anybody?" pleaded the auctioneer. But no matter how hard he tried, the auctioneer couldn't get anybody else to bid.

"Sold for $500 to bidder number 61."

"Oh no, I forgot," said Heather in a panicked voice. "Did you get a number?"

"No, I thought you'd get one," replied Laura.

"Shoot. Now what do I do? My mare is the next lot."

"Just bid, I'll go get one," said Laura as she jumped up from her seat and disappeared into the crowd.

Now Heather wasn't just excited, but nervous also. She was no longer able to sit quietly in her old, uncomfortable chair. Instead she moved around, first sitting on her hands, then slouching, once again using her hands as a seat and finally sitting at attention as she saw the little gray mare being led in.

"Here's a cutie for you, folks," bellowed the auctioneer. "I don't know a lot about her, only that she's just a youngster and hasn't been worked much. My form says she's a registered Morgan, but I've never seen a gray Morgan so maybe that isn't right. But that doesn't matter, as she's so nice. You don't want to miss this chance to get a nice, four-year-old mare and train her the way you like. Who wants to start the bidding at $1500?"

Just like the previous horse, nobody seemed particularly interested in this animal. Heather looked around nervously, trying to catch a glimpse of the first bidder. But she didn't see a single hand rise, or a single voice shout out in excitement. The horse seemed nervous too as she paced around and around, unwilling to stand still. The handler tried to get her to pose in front of the crowd, but she refused, instead giving out an ear-piercing cry as she began to paw the ground.

"Are you sure you want her?" asked Laura as she returned to her seat. "She seems pretty antsy to me. Oh, I forgot, here's your number."

Laura handed Heather a small piece of white cardboard with the number '82' handwritten on it and a large tongue-depressor glued to the back side which apparently was to be used as a handle.

"Come on folks," interrupted the auctioneer. "What are you waiting for? You won't see a better horse today, and you're going to kick yourselves when you have to drive home without this handsome horse in your trailer. Do I hear $800? $800 anybody?"

Laura looked at her friend. "Aren't you going to bid? What are you waiting for?"

"I'm going to wait until the very last minute. I want to get her for the lowest price possible."

"Well, don't wait too long or you won't get her at all!"

"$450!"

Both girls turned to see who had just bid. A middle-aged man sitting several rows behind them, with greasy, shoulder length black hair and whose large stomach was probably the result of far too many trips to the local fast-food restaurant, had his hand raised.

"I have $450! Do I hear $500?" shouted the auctioneer who seemed relieved to have finally gotten a bid. "Hey Jim," he continued, "tack her up and let's show these folks what a nice riding horse she is."

There was a brief pause in the action as one of the assistants got up from a nearby seat to do what he was told. Jim was a man of perhaps thirty, with long, matted hair like so many of the other workers at the auction. He wore a blue and white flannel shirt that was worn through at the elbows, jeans that were worn through at the knees and boots that needed to be thrown out. The young man looked slightly annoyed at the thought of riding the horse, but he obediently grabbed a western saddle that had been lying on the ground near the auctioneer and rather roughly tossed it onto the young mare's back. The frightened horse jumped slightly as the saddle landed on her back and her ears flattened against her neck to show her displeasure. Jim didn't bother to put a blanket between the saddle and the horse, and as soon as the saddle was on, he turned towards the auctioneer with a quizzical look on his face.

"Where's her bridle?" asked the assistant.

"Oh, here, use this one," replied another helper from the sidelines. An old, worn-out looking bridle was tossed to Jim, the assistant trying to tack up the horse. Jim reached for the bridle, but missed it and it flopped to the ground. He picked it up, brushed off some dirt from the piece of equipment and returned to the mare. In less than a minute he had the bridle on the horse and had climbed aboard.

"Okay, now folks, watch this pretty little mare and let's get the bidding going!" shouted the auctioneer as he tried to get the audience excited about the horse.

Jim had every intention of making the horse look as enticing as possible, but the little mare had other ideas. The bit that had been forced into her mouth was old, rusty and had several sharp edges along the inside that cut into her mouth with each pull of the reins. The mare pinned her ears back, lowered her head and started to back up in an attempt to escape from the pain that the bit was causing.

"I think she's going to buck!" exclaimed Laura.

"No, look at her face," said Heather. "She doesn't look mean, she looks scared. I bet that rider is pulling too hard on the reins. Or maybe the bit is one she's never had in her mouth before. Look, it's a curb bit. Isn't that kind of rough for a young horse?"

"It can be, if used wrong. But then again, pretty much any bit can hurt if used wrong," replied Laura.

With a couple of good, hard kicks, Jim managed to get the mare walking forward. She walked slowly, cocking her head towards the crowd and cautiously looking at them. At one point she stopped, raised her head and snorted loudly at somebody sitting in the front row. But a quick kick from her rider got her going again.

"Okay folks, do I hear $500? Come on now, she's a bit green but we can all see that she'll make a great riding horse with a little work. And what a broodmare she'll make in the future! $500, do I hear $500?"

Deciding that it was time to act, Heather raised her hand.

"$500, do I hear $500?" continued the auctioneer. Apparently he didn't see Heather's hand.

"Here, here!" shouted the girl, anxious to get her bid heard.

"We have $500 over there," yelled the auctioneer, looking at the far end of the arena. Everyone, including Heather, turned to look at the bidder. A young man, perhaps in his early twenties, had his hand up and was smiling.

"We have $500, do I hear $600?"

Heather's hand shot up in an instant and this time she didn't wait. She yelled out "here" as loudly as she could.

"I've got $600 over there," continued the auctioneer, this time looking at Heather. "How about $700? You know she's worth the price," encouraged the auctioneer, turning his attention to the other two bidders.

The middle-aged man shook his head back and forth to signal his desire to stop bidding. The auctioneer then turned his attention to the younger gentleman.

"How high are you going to go?" whispered Laura.

"I don't know. I can't go much higher." Heather looked at the mare, who seemed to have relaxed just a bit. Her rider gave the horse yet another kick and the mare broke into a tense, nervous looking trot. When she got to the end of the ring, she stumbled as she tried to turn tightly and trot at the same time. For her effort, she received two heels snapped sharply into her sides.

$650!" hollered the young man who was bidding against Heather.

"Don't up the bid right away. Wait till the very last minute," advised Laura.

"$700?" asked the auctioneer, looking at Heather.

"$700!" came a woman's voice. Heather turned to see a well-dressed woman, several rows behind her.

"I have $700, do I hear $800?" asked the auctioneer.

Silence filled the arena. Somebody coughed. Heather's right leg started doing a quick little up and down motion, a habit that frequently showed itself when she was tense.

"What should I do?" she whispered to her friend.

"Wait, wait," came the reply.

"$800, $800. Do I hear $800?"

A short pause that seemed to last forever followed.

"Going once for $700..."

27

"$800!" shouted Heather.

"Twice, wait, we have another bid. $800 from the young lady. Anybody else?"

Another brief pause followed as the auctioneer looked into the crowd, trying to find another bidder.

"I have $800. Do I hear $850?"

Heather's stomach twisted in knots, awaiting the outcome.

"$800, going once, twice, sold!" shouted the auctioneer as he slammed his gavel down on the podium. "Your number please."

Heather held up her little, hand-made placard.

"Lot number eighteen, sold to bidder number 82 for $800. Thank you ma'am. Now look what we have here, a gorgeous bay Thoroughbred that I'm told easily jumps four foot fences and has been started in training-level dressage."

Heather and Laura got up and began to make their way to the office. The little mare was led away, presumably back to the small pasture where Heather had first met her.

CHAPTER THREE

GETTING ACQUAINTED

"What are you going to call her?" asked Laura.

"I don't know. How about 'Frosty'? That's a cool name for a gray horse," replied Heather.

"Yeah, I like that!" said Laura. The two girls had been chatting up a storm all the way home from the auction. Heather was so excited about her new horse that she just couldn't contain herself. She thought about how well the scared little mare had behaved when they met for the second time following the sale. After paying for the horse, they had proceeded to the pen where the gray mare was being held. They haltered her with the only halter available, a horrible nylon contraption that really belonged in the trash and led the mare out of the pen towards their truck and trailer. The sweet horse had loaded into the trailer after only a few minutes of coaxing and although a bit nervous, didn't give her new owner any trouble. Closing up the trailer, the young friends hopped into the truck and headed for home.

"What are you going to do with her?" asked Laura.

"Oh, gee, I hadn't even thought about that! I'd love to show her, maybe take her to some Morgan shows. Do you really think she's a Morgan?"

"It's possible," answered Laura. "The salesperson did tell you that she was. But of course, they have to send you the registration papers. That sounds a little weird to me. Why wouldn't they have them there at the auction? And why on earth would anyone get rid of a gray Morgan? They're so unusual. I'd think they're pretty special, and you'd certainly want to keep such a horse if you had one. I guess you'll know soon enough. That guy in the office told you the papers would be mailed from the original owner within a week."

The truck was filled with chatter as it pulled into the yard of Gallant Morgan Horse Farm. The farm consisted of a barn, hidden from the road slightly by several large maple trees, and a ranch style house painted barn red, which was set apart from the barn by a small hill. As the truck came to a stop in front of the barn, a loud whinny of greeting immediately shot out from the barn.

"Hi Blackjack!" shouted Heather as she got out of the truck.

A second whinny came from the barn, although it was in a higher pitch.

"Yes, Rusty, I know you're in the barn too!"

As Heather shouted her greeting to Rusty, another whinny, this time from the trailer, was heard.

"I guess everyone knows we're here," laughed Laura.

"Well, well. What do you have in the trailer?" came a voice from the barn. Heather smiled as she saw Chauncy saunter out of the barn, his gray hair hidden under a cap. This kindly old man, whose hands and face were weathered from all the harsh New England winters that they had endured, was always a welcome sight. The young horse enthusiast considered him a second father, for he had taught her so much about horses, and always did so with patience and a smile on his face.

"Remember how you said you'd like to start filling your barn up with horses?" asked Heather, with a sly grin on her face.

"What did you buy?" inquired Chauncy, knowing that there was a horse hidden inside the trailer.

"Come look!" said Heather as she led Chauncy over to the trailer.

They walked over to the vehicle and Heather cautiously opened the side door so that they could peer in. As Chauncy leaned forward to see what surprise was held within the confines of the trailer, a gray muzzle pushed its way out.

"Well, hello there!" greeted Chauncy.

"What do you think? Do you like her?" eagerly asked Heather.

"It's pretty hard to tell from this angle. Why don't we take her out and have a look?"

Chauncy and Heather walked around to the back of the trailer, opened the door and lowered the ramp. The mare, eager to get out and explore her new surroundings, obediently took instructions from her new owner and was quickly unloaded from the trailer. As soon as she was completely off the vehicle, the young horse raised her head high into the air and let out an ear-piercing scream. Blackjack and Rusty, confined to their stalls and unable to see this visitor, both let out equally loud squeals. Frosty, just as eager to meet her new stablemates, let out a second scream. She then froze in place and let out several short snorts, as if she was trying to blow something out of her nose. With her head held high, ears pricked forward, tail held out away from her body, and not a single muscle moving, Heather thought her new horse looked absolutely stunning.

"She's just like a statue, isn't she? What do you think, do you like her?" asked Heather, anxious for confirmation from her mentor that this was indeed a nice horse.

"Well how the heck did you get your hands on a gray Morgan?" asked a perplexed Chauncy. "There aren't very many left in the breed and I'm surprised that anybody would sell one."

"I wasn't even sure she was a Morgan," admitted Heather. "She sure looks like one but I didn't know Morgans came in gray."

"What's her breeding?"

"I don't know. Her registration papers are going to be mailed to me so I haven't seen them."

"Well, by looking at her, I'd say you've got some Brunk breeding in there. Maybe a touch of Government too," guessed Chauncy as he walked around Frosty, looking her over carefully. "I like her," he finally said. "She's got a real nice head, nice, sloping shoulder, good topline and solid, straight legs. I think she'll make a real nice horse."

Relieved that Chauncy, who could pick out conformation related problems that others rarely noticed, approved of her horse, Heather gave Frosty a big pat on her neck. Just as she did so, the mare let out yet another scream.

"Guess they want to meet each other!" said Heather, a big smile on her face. "Come on Frosty, let's go say 'hi' to your new friends."

"Oh, no, not so fast," cautioned Chauncy. "You can't just introduce her to the other horses. You don't know where she has been, what trailers she's ridden in, the horses that she's met. She could be carrying any number of diseases from a simple cold to something much more serious. No nose sniffing for her, at least for a couple of weeks. Laura, would you put some bedding in that stall at the far end of the barn, please?"

"But it's so far away from the others," complained Heather. "Can't she be in the stall next to Rusty?"

"Do you really want Rusty to get sick? He's nineteen now and too old to risk exposure to any infections. Don't worry, your new girl will be fine."

Heather reluctantly led Frosty towards the barn. The bottom half of the building was made of cinder blocks while the upper half was wood, which was painted barn red to match the house. There was a single large sliding door at the front, which was kept open during the day for ventilation. The inside had a tack room near the entrance and five stalls on each side. Like the outside, each stall had cinder blocks on the bottom half and wood above it, although the inside wood was oak, which was much nicer than the pine used on the outside. Each stall had a simple wooden door and because there were no top sections to them, both Blackjack and Rusty had their heads poking out, straining against the doors in an effort to get closer to their new friend. The stalled horses were each in the third stall, Blackjack on the right side and Rusty on the left. With heads out and noses reaching as far towards Frosty as possible, it looked too frightening for the timid mare. Although there was plenty of room for Heather and Frosty to get through, the mare wasn't convinced and she certainly wasn't going to go forward. As she approached, she stopped in her tracks with a look of fear in her eyes.

"Don't worry girl, they won't hurt you. They just like to talk," consoled Heather.

"Here, let me help," offered Laura, as she walked over to Rusty and gently pushed his head into his stall. Blocking his view, Laura kept her position until Heather passed. Laura had put the bedding in the last stall on Rusty's side of the barn and so that's where Heather led her new horse. Once in the stall, Heather took the old, tattered nylon halter off Frosty and left the stall.

Closing the door, she said, to no one in particular, "I think I'm going to have a lot of fun with Frosty. She's a cool horse and I can't wait to show her."

Frosty, oblivious to the attention she was getting, was fixated on the sweet smelling shavings that had just been placed in her new stall. With head lowered, she circled around and around, much like a dog who is trying to find a perfect place to lie down. Finally, with a loud groan, she slowly fell to her knees and then laid down, smack in the middle of the shavings. She rubbed her neck against the floor several times, in obvious satisfaction and then rolled over once, twice, then three times. The third time her front hooves hit the wall and made a loud thunking noise. The mare again rubbed her neck against the floor, hesitated for just a moment and then got up. Once

"...as Frosty approached, she stopped in her tracks with a look of fear in her eyes."

on her feet, she kept her head lowered and shook her whole body, perhaps in an attempt to get the shavings out of her mane and tail. She snorted and walked towards her new owner. As the mare approached, Heather burst out laughing. Although Frosty had managed to rid herself of many of the shavings that had attached to her mane and tail, there were still quite a few shavings stuck to her whiskers.

"You look ridiculous!" laughed Heather as she reached past the closed stall door to the approaching horse. Frosty stopped directly in front of Heather, and while leaning against the door, began rubbing her neck against the girl's side. She rubbed so hard that Heather had to grab the door with her hands to keep from falling over.

"Okay, that's enough. Here, have some hay," said Laura as she tossed a flake of hay over the door. Frosty attacked the hay as though she had not eaten in a week. Her tail slowly swished back and forth to keep the first few flies of spring at bay.

****

Heather's parents, much to her relief, were pleased with her new purchase. Mr. and Mrs. Richardson were extremely supportive of their daughter's passionate love of horses and encouraged her whenever possible. Although they had once been reluctant to allow her to spend time with Blackjack, when they saw how determined their daughter was, and how she managed to keep her grades up in school, they relented. Knowing that falling behind in school might limit her involvement with horses, Heather always worked very hard in school. Once she decided that she wanted another horse, Heather knew she'd have to get her parents' approval. They discussed at length the responsibilities that having a second horse would bring and had insisted that Heather earn half of the money to pay for the horse herself. It took all winter, but by doing extra chores around the barn and working at the school store as much as possible, Heather eventually earned $450 and received permission to start her horse hunt.

On the way home from the barn, Heather's mom suggested stopping off at the tack shop to buy Frosty a new halter. Heather eagerly agreed and found a lovely, all-leather halter with a brass nameplate. When the clerk offered to engrave the nameplate at no charge, Heather was thrilled. The halter would look great on that beautiful gray head.

The next morning Heather arrived at the barn bright and early. The first show of the season was next weekend and she and Blackjack needed to practice. Of course, her eagerness to get to the barn was primarily because she wanted to see her new horse. So, after getting up very early, doing chores and going to church, Heather got her mom to drop her off well before lunch. The young horse lover rushed into the barn, ran into Blackjack's stall to give him a big hug and then proceeded to Frosty's stall.

"Hi girl, how are you doing?" she asked, peering into the stall.

The horse looked up from her hay, snorted and then returned her attention to her meal.

"I guess you're hungry. Well, I'll let you eat while I clean up the barn a little."

"Don't I get a 'hello' today?" asked a voice.

Heather turned to see Chauncy enter the barn.

"Oh, I'm sorry. I didn't see you."

"That's okay, I was actually in the house. Mrs. Campbell is going to be making her homemade chicken soup today. I assume you'll be staying for lunch?"

"Sure, I'd love to, if you don't mind."

Chauncy laughed at the thought. His wife, Mrs. Campbell, obviously loved having Heather over for lunch and would be upset if the girl didn't stop by the house. With her own children all grown, Mrs. Campbell lavished all sorts of motherly attention on Heather. Like Chauncy, Heather considered her family.

"I'll tell her to put an extra plate on the table when I go back up to the house in a little while," said Chauncy. Then, changing the subject, he asked, "Are you going to work Blackjack?"

"Yeah, I think I better. The show is just a week away and we need to work on our road trot just a little bit."

Heather went over to Blackjack's stall, grabbed his halter from the stall door and walked into the horse's stall.

"Hey there, what's up?" she quietly said to her favorite horse. Blackjack was a stunning animal and he knew it. He was large for a Morgan, standing a solid 15.2 hands and was all black, with the exception of a small half-moon tuft of white hair on his forehead. His long forelock, which almost touched his nose, completely covered the white marking on his head. The thing that drew Heather to this horse, however, was not all of his outer beauty but rather his heart and kindness. Chauncy had said that you could always tell a kind horse by looking at his eyes. If the eyes were big, soft and expressive, then the horse would be gentle and sweet natured. In contrast, he said, little, squinty, pig-eyed horses tended to be mean and cranky. That's why Heather had been so drawn to Frosty; so many of the other horses at the auction had tiny, little eyes with pinned back ears. Frosty, however, had those great big Morgan eyes that just begged for attention. As for Blackjack, he had the biggest, softest, melt-your-heart eyes Heather had ever seen. He was always eager for attention and would even stop eating his grain for the chance to spend time with Heather.

Heather slipped the halter onto Blackjack's head and led him out of the stall and up to the front of the barn where all the grooming was done. Eager to start riding, Heather brushed her horse, tacked him up, grabbed her hardhat and brought her horse outside to the riding ring. As she was about to get on Blackjack, Frosty let out a squeal. Blackjack turned his attention towards the barn, head held high, frozen in place. A muscle on his shoulder twitched as a fly attempted to land on him.

"Come on boy, never mind that. Let's get to work," advised Heather as she climbed aboard. Unlike most of her friends who rode their horses either western or huntseat, Heather rode Blackjack saddleseat. Other riders would stare at her long, flat saddle and bridle with two bits and two sets of reins with a quizzical look, but she just loved saddleseat. The fancy, high-stepping horses, the surging power of the animal beneath her, eager to move on, the elegant formal attire that she wore when showing were all things that Heather treasured.

Heather couldn't wait until next week's show, the first of the season. They were going to compete in the road hack class, Heather's favorite. It was a class that asked for more speed than many of the other classes and that's what she loved about it. It was a challenge and it was fun! Today they were going to practice getting that speed without sacrificing their proper form.

The pair spent several minutes walking around, first this way and then that. Blackjack, although interested, seemed a bit lazy today. But as soon as Heather gathered up her reins, signaling to her horse that it was time to get to work, he woke up. Blackjack collected himself, drawing his hind end up beneath himself and raising his neck in a proud arch. His walk became more animated, with his knees reaching higher and his pace quickening just a bit. Heather tapped her heels gently against the sides of her horse and Blackjack obediently picked up a trot. He was eager to go and although he was totally controlled, he felt as though he might explode at any moment. Heather loved the feeling; all that power and strength beneath her, but instead of fighting against her, the two were working as a pair. She felt like a princess on her gallant steed.

After trotting around at a somewhat collected pleasure trot, Heather clucked to her horse. She wanted him to move out into a road trot, a faster, more extended trot. Blackjack immediately turned on the speed. The Morgan breed developed fantastic trots due to its use as a harness horse before the rise of the automobile, and this trait was passed down to many of today's Morgans. Blackjack was no exception as his road trot was so fast that he could easily keep up with many horses that were cantering. He loved to fly around the ring at speed, and sometimes he went so fast that

Heather had trouble posting to the quickened beat of his trot. As Blackjack flew around the ring, he began to lean forward just a tiny bit so Heather adjusted her top rein to get him to collect just a little more. A few more times around the ring and the rider brought her horse back down to a walk.

Next came the canter, a nice, collected, rocking horse gait. A few times around the ring and then Heather once again urged her horse on, asking for a hand gallop. This faster gait was also a requirement of the road hack class. She leaned forward slightly and loosened the reins a little. Blackjack once again extended his gait, but this time he managed to maintain his frame and not get strung out like he had at the road trot. Heather only asked her horse to hand gallop once around the ring as she didn't want to get him too excited or too tired. Bringing him back to a walk, she gave him a huge pat and told him what a good boy he was. They reversed directions and continued the workout.

After Blackjack had been cooled out and returned to his stall, Heather turned her attention to Frosty. The mare had been hanging her head out of her stall, watching every little movement, learning about her surroundings. She obediently lowered her head for the halter and followed Heather to the front of the barn. Once there, Heather snapped the cross ties onto either side of Frosty's halter and got to work cleaning the mare up. The caked on mud and gunk came off fairly easily with a plastic curry comb. The mare seemed to enjoy the attention and particularly liked it when her new friend was working on the underside of her neck. As Heather rubbed and rubbed with the comb, Frosty raised her neck and head up into the air, in total delight. Her upper lip curled up and she appeared to be smiling.

"You like that, huh?" asked Heather. "Bet you haven't been clean in a very long time."

As she worked towards the back of the horse, Heather lightened the pressure, not wanting to annoy the horse as she brushed more sensitive areas. Once the body was relatively clean (and Heather was relatively dirty from all the flying dust and dirt), she switched brushes. A softer brush was needed for the legs. One particularly encrusted area of dirt on a back leg required some extra effort and Frosty, at one point, raised her leg in displeasure. Other than that small incident, the cleaning went along quietly. Heather was relieved to find that Frosty had no trouble picking up her feet for cleaning. The young horsewoman knew that a horse that doesn't like its legs touched could be rather dangerous when it comes to hoof care.

Once the body and legs were clean, Heather set about getting the burrs out of the mane, forelock and tail. She tried using the plastic curry comb but that just made more of a mess. Reluctantly, she put the comb down and began separating a few hairs at a time from the burrs with her hands. It was a very time consuming process and Heather found herself thinking that cutting all the hair off really wouldn't be that bad. Of course, Frosty would sure look funny.

After what seemed like an eternity, the last burr was pulled out of the tail and although rather frizzy, the mane, forelock and tail looked much better. To finish the job, Heather used her softest brush to go all around Frosty's body, getting off every last remnant of dirt. As she approached the mare's head, Frosty again started to curl her upper lip and it was then that Heather noticed the blisters inside the horse's mouth.

"What is that?" she asked herself.

Heather gently raised the mare's lip and could see three blister-like areas along the topside of the lip, and two on the lower half. Each disfigured area was about the size of a dime and oblong in shape. Checking the other side of her mouth, Heather found identical scabs.

"Chauncy, where are you?" she called out. "I need you to look at something."

"I'm in Rusty's stall. I'll be right there," came the reply.

In a moment, Chauncy appeared.

"What's wrong?" he asked.

"Take a look at these," said Heather as she lifted Frosty's lip again and showed Chauncy the blisters. "What are they?"

Chauncy took a careful look at the area in question and then gently felt the blisters with his thumb. Frosty didn't seem to mind at all.

"They don't seem to hurt her, so what could they be? Did she somehow burn herself? Maybe eat something that was bad? Rub her lips on a fence that had poison on it?" asked Heather, trying to figure out what it could be.

"I haven't see this in a long, long time," began Chauncy. "This is a sign that your horse is infested with worms. These blister-like areas are worm larvae that are migrating through the lips."

"Oh! Gross! Gross! Gross!" exclaimed Heather. "That is so disgusting. Oh, gross!"

"Don't worry, it's nothing that a little wormer can't take care of," said Chauncy as he disappeared into the tack room. A moment later he reappeared with a long, white plastic syringe.

Inserting one end into Frosty's mouth, he depressed the other end and dispensed a dose of wormer into the horse. "There, all set. She'll be fine."

Heather looked somewhat dumbfounded. What she had just found was absolutely disgusting and the fact that somebody would neglect their horse by not worming it was even more upsetting.

"I was going to lunge her today, Chauncy. Should I just put her back in her stall instead?" shouted Heather to her mentor, who had once again disappeared into Rusty's stall.

Poking his head out of the stall, Chauncy replied, "No, you don't need to put her back. Just work her lightly today. Walk her a bit and maybe let her trot for just a few minutes. That will be enough for the first day."

Glad that she had gotten the okay to work the horse, Heather attached a lunge line to the underside of Frosty's halter, grabbed her lunge whip and led the horse outside. There was a small, grassy, level area next to the barn where she always did her lunge line work, and it was here that she led Frosty. Amongst the grass was a circular path made from years of horses walking around and around. Walking to the middle of the circle, Heather let out the line and asked Frosty to move out to the path. The mare just stood there and looked at Heather.

"No, I want you to go out to the path, silly."

The mare looked at Heather.

"Well, this isn't going to work," sighed Heather. She led Frosty to the path, then turned and walked back to the center. Frosty followed her back to the center.

"No, no, no. That's not right," scolded Heather, a bit louder but not yet frustrated. "You have to go out there," she said as she once again led her horse to the path.

This time, as Heather returned, she kept on eye on the horse to ensure that the mare wouldn't follow her.

Frosty just stood there, watching Heather return to the center.

"Good, now walk," commanded Heather.

Frosty didn't move.

"Come on girl, let's get going," encouraged Heather.

Frosty continued to look at her, not moving a muscle.

Heather clucked to the horse. Nothing. She raised her whip, which she never hit the horse with but instead used as a guide and gently tapped Frosty on the hind end. Frosty took several steps forward.

"Good girl, that's it!"

Frosty stopped.

"No, girl. You have to keep moving."

Heather once again tapped the horse gently on her rump. Frosty turned and started walking towards the center.

"No, that's not it. Come on, let's follow the path."

But Frosty continued walking toward Heather. In a moment she was standing next to the girl. The young trainer sighed and led Frosty back out to the path.

"Let's try this one more time," she suggested.

Raising the whip, once again as a guide, Heather encouraged the horse to move along the path. After several more unsuccessful attempts,

Frosty finally figured it out and stayed on the path. Five minutes later Heather stopped the horse and asked her to reverse. Once again, totally confused, Frosty just stood there, looking at her trainer. Heather was forced to help the mare change directions and it took a few false starts before the horse was once again moving along properly. A few more minutes and Heather called it quits for the day.

"I don't think she's ever been lunged," announced Heather as she returned to the barn.

"I was watching you out there and I'd have to say you're right," agreed Chauncy. "She didn't have a clue what to do. But did you notice that she didn't get upset or mean? That's very important. She may not be trained very well but at least she's willing to learn."

****

The following week flew by. Heather was busy at school, having been swamped with homework. Meanwhile, after school each day she'd take the bus to Chauncy's so that she could get Blackjack ready for the show and continue to work Frosty. By the end of the week, the blister-like marks on Frosty's lips had almost completely disappeared and she had settled into her new home nicely. Blackjack was going well and Heather was confident that they'd do great at the show. Frosty learned how to lunge quickly, and by Friday, Heather felt ready to ride her. She knew the mare was broke to saddle, having seen her ridden at the auction. Lunging her had been a great way to get the mare used to Heather, see how she reacted to a saddle on her back as she trotted around (she hardly noticed it) and to study the mare's work habits. Heather's conclusion was that with a little work, Frosty would be a spectacular mare and take the show world by storm. But before that could happen, the horse would have to be ridden.

After lunging Frosty for about fifteen minutes to loosen her up, Heather brought her into the barn to tack her up for riding.

"What bridle should I use?" she asked as she tacked up her horse.

"Let's use the snaffle. We want to take it easy on her," suggested Chauncy.

When the bridle was put on, Frosty seemed to get a little upset. She started pawing the ground, her ears went back slightly and she raised and lowered her head several times.

"Is it too tight?" asked Heather.

Chauncy checked the fit of the bridle and bit.

"No, it looks fine. Maybe she's just a tad nervous. Take her out to the ring."

Heather grabbed her riding helmet from the tack room and then led Frosty out of the barn. As soon as they got to the gate, the mare stopped.

"Come on girl," said Heather, encouragingly. "We're just going to work in the ring. It's no big deal."

But Frosty was not convinced. She planted her feet firmly in place and raised her head in defiance. Chauncy, who had been following the pair from a short distance, used his voice to try to get the mare to enter the ring but it had no effect. As Heather continued gently pulling on the reins and talking to her horse, Chauncy, who was now standing beside the mare, reached out and tapped the mare's hind end with his hand. The only effect this had was to make the gray mare take a step backwards.

"Heather," instructed Chauncy, "turn her around."

"Huh? What will that do, Chauncy? I want to get her into the ring, not go back to the barn."

"Trust me," encouraged her instructor.

Heather turned Frosty around, which was easy as the mare was very willing to turn towards the barn.

"Now back her up," said Chauncy.

Heather gently pulled back on the reins and the mare obediently backed up. Before Frosty realized it, she was in the ring. Heather turned her horse around and walked to the center of the ring.

"What was that all about?" she asked Frosty.

As Heather pulled her stirrups down and adjusted the girth, Frosty once again pawed at the ground and threw her head up and down.

"Why is she so agitated?" asked Heather.

"I don't know," admitted Chauncy. "Maybe she's had a bad experience in a ring. Just take it real easy and slow, okay?"

"Sure, I don't want to push her."

Heather gave the girth one final check and then, while Chauncy held the reins, she put on her riding helmet and mounted. Gathering up her reins, the rider asked the horse to walk over to the rail. Hesitating for just a moment, Frosty reluctantly began to walk. But unlike Blackjack or Rusty, who enjoyed being ridden and walked in a quick yet relaxed way, Frosty walked very slowly, as if she had to think about each step she was taking. Her neck was quite high but her head, which should have been bent over at the poll so that her nose slanted towards the ground, was instead held high, as if she were trying to look at the sun. Every muscle was tense and Heather wasn't sure what the mare would do, walk or try to run away.

"She's really uptight," remarked Heather.

"Just relax and hopefully she will too," said Chauncy. "Keep her on the rail and see if you can get her to calm down. And don't forget to talk to her!"

Heather continued to circle the ring, all the while telling Frosty what a wonderful horse she was, how they were going to have so much fun and of all the great shows they were going to go to. After numerous trips around the ring Frosty began to relax but Heather could still tell that she was tense.

"Try a slow, easy trot," said Chauncy.

Heather, not wanting to upset the mare, first tried using her voice, instead of her legs, to urge the mare on. The only response she got from Frosty was that she changed her flat-footed walk into a jig, something between a walk and a trot. Another cluck and more jigging. Heather reluctantly used her legs, squeezing with her upper legs and tapping with her heels. Frosty immediately broke into a very fast trot, much too fast for Heather.

"Easy girl, slow down," said Heather as she tightened her reins. But Frosty didn't listen. She continued to race, head held high as if she were looking for stars, neck muscles tense and nostrils flared. She shook her head up and down, up and down, trying to evade the bit pressure, although the reins were not being held very tightly. Unable to escape from whatever threat she perceived, Frosty tried going faster and faster. Heather, forced to tighten her reins once again to keep the mare from running away, felt her own body begin to tense up.

"Try circling her at the far end of the ring," suggested Chauncy.

As they approached the area where they were to circle, Frosty continued to fight the rein pressure. Heather asked her to turn in towards the center of the ring, so that they could circle and Frosty fought that too. Her neck arched away from the center, and her nose was turned as far as possible toward the rail. As they made their turn, the mare's head and neck continued in their awkward position while her body was forced to slant inwards to compensate for the unwieldy angle of the upper body. This whole movement made it difficult for the horse to see where she was going and so, in the middle of her circle, she tripped. Caught off-guard, Heather was flung forward by the motion and was forced to grab her horse's mane to keep from falling off. Frosty, however, seemed to ignore her rider's problems as she concentrated on regaining her stride and continuing on in her struggle.

Once the circle was completed, the pair continued around the ring, with the mare doing everything to get away from whatever imagined fear was chasing her while her rider tried to comfort her. A few more passes around the ring and Heather asked Frosty to come back to a walk. The mare returned to her nervous jig, only this time she was breathing hard and sweating.

"I'd say you have a very ring sour horse," observed Chauncy. "Somebody really messed her up because there was no reason for her bad behavior other than fear. I think you are going to have a very difficult time retraining her..."

CHAPTER FOUR

THE SHOW

The following morning, Heather arrived at the barn at seven o'clock. She needed to give Blackjack a final cleaning before loading him into the trailer and wanted to spend a little time with Frosty too. Hopping out of the car, she kissed her mom goodbye and grabbed her formal show outfit from out of the back seat.

"I'll call you when I get back, okay Mom?"

"That's fine honey. Your dad and I are going out and won't be back until three. So don't panic if you call and we're not there."

"Oh, I don't think we'll be back until dinner."

"Okay, good luck!" said Mrs. Richardson as she drove off.

"Hey Laura, are you ready for a fun day?" asked Heather as she approached the truck. Laura was busy hooking the trailer to the pickup and hadn't seen Heather approach.

"Oh, hey there. Yeah, it should be great. The weather is supposed to be really nice."

Heather opened the door to the truck and carefully placed her show clothes, contained in a garment bag, on the front seat. Then she headed to the barn to see her horses. Walking into Blackjack's stall, she was greeted with a soft nicker. Her horse was just finishing his breakfast and was searching for any stray tidbits of hay that he might have missed. With amazing dexterity, Blackjack's nose moved along the floor, sniffing here and there, and wiggling around any little strand of hay that it found until the food disappeared into his mouth.

"I think you've got it all," noted Heather.

Determined that there must still be a little food left, Blackjack continued his search. Heather meanwhile, buried her head in his neck, feeling his warmth and taking in the wonderful aroma of horse.

"We're going to have a fun day," she finally said as she patted him and left his stall.

Turning her attention to Frosty, Heather walked over to her stall. Frosty looked up from her hay and greeted her owner. With several strands of hay hanging down from her forelock, she looked rather comical. Pulling the hay out of her hair, Heather smiled at her new horse.

"I wish I knew what got you so upset in the ring yesterday, Frosty. Somebody must have really hurt you to make you so nervous. I promise I'll never hurt you but you're going to have to learn to trust me."

Heather went up to the tack room, found a soft curry brush and returned to Frosty. Entering the stall, she began to brush the horse. Frosty stood perfectly still, her eyes almost shut. She obviously enjoyed the sensation of the brush and the attention she was getting. Heather, finding a spot of dried dirt on the mare's back, gave that area a little extra attention. As she vigorously brushed away the dirt, Frosty turned her head to face Heather and began to nuzzle the girl's back.

The harder Heather brushed, the harder Frosty nuzzled. At first it tickled, but soon Heather found herself arching her back to alleviate some of the pressure from Frosty's nose. Removing the last speck of dirt, Heather stopped brushing and, in return, Frosty stopped her grooming.

"Geez, you are just so sweet. How on earth did you get so messed up and manage to keep your wonderful attitude at the same time?"

Frosty just looked at Heather. Giving her mare a big hug, the girl left Frosty's stall and turned her attention back to Blackjack and the upcoming show.

****

Heather, Laura and Blackjack arrived at the Morgan show a couple of hours before the road hack class. The fairgrounds where the show was held was a popular place, where many different events, for all types of horses, took place. Numerous barns, with countless stalls, a huge indoor arena, a large outdoor ring as well as a big infield where jumping and carriage driving classes were held, filled the fairgrounds. During large events, all the stalls would be filled and sometimes even temporary, tent-like barns would be erected to hold all the horses. But this was the first show of the season, and not a lot of horses came. There were plenty of stalls to choose from and the classes tended to be small.

The two girls first went to the show office where they picked up Heather's number and then returned to put Blackjack into a stall. Once settled in his stall, eating a flake of hay, Heather and Laura wandered off to find some lunch. These shows always had one or two vendors selling really bad, overpriced food. Tiny little hamburgers,

53

greasy fries and hotdogs that had been sitting on the grill too long were in high demand. Heather had to force herself to eat a hamburger since she normally got very nervous before her class and found eating rather difficult. Once lunch was over, the two friends returned to Blackjack and, while Heather got dressed in her formal attire, Laura put the finishing touches on the horse.

"Ten minutes to class 57, Road Hack, Amateur to Ride," announced the voice over the speakers.

"Are you ready?" asked Laura, as she pulled Blackjack out of the stall. As the horse stepped out into the sunlight, his hooves, now sporting black hoof polish, glistened in the bright light. His coat, which had been vigorously cleaned and sprayed with conditioners, was absolutely beautiful, while his tail, which had been carefully combed to remove every single knot, flowed down to the ground. Heather, meanwhile, appeared from the next stall, a stall that she had used as a dressing room. Now she looked like a much more mature version of herself. Her hair was pulled back into the required bun; she wore a formal dress jacket with tails, perfectly matched pants, shiny, black boots and a derby upon her head. The dark colored gloves hid the dirt on her hands, dirt that she hadn't had time to wash off before she got dressed.

"He looks great," complimented Heather.

"Have a fantastic ride!" encouraged Laura as she helped her friend, constrained in her formal attire, onto the horse.

Heather gathered up her reins and was about to ask her horse to move along when

Blackjack suddenly jerked his head up and took five rather awkward steps backwards.

"Hey, what's that all about?" asked Heather as she used her legs to get Blackjack's attention. "You're not trying to get out of work, are you?"

"He's probably just being lazy. Walk him around a bit and let him loosen up," suggested Laura.

Heather clucked to her horse and gave him a kick. After a moment's hesitation, Blackjack started walking forward. They walked towards the outdoor ring and within a few minutes, the brief disobedience of the animal was forgotten as the tension of the upcoming class grew. They arrived at the warm-up ring, an area next to the main ring that was used by those getting ready to compete. While Laura watched from the side, Heather collected her reins and asked Blackjack to trot along the rail. With over a dozen riders in the ring going both ways, and even a few cutting across the middle, doing circles or suddenly stopping, it took a bit of skill to guide her horse through the crowd. Blackjack seemed to feel the tension and excitement that was building as he started to trot higher and higher, raising his neck just a little bit, as if to say 'look at me!' Heather wanted to save her horse's energy for the class, so she didn't ask him to do too much. A little trotting to get him warmed up was enough for her so after a short workout, she asked Blackjack to walk. Then, as the results of the class before road hack were announced, Heather leaned over, gave her horse a huge pat and said, "Okay Blackjack, this is it. Let's go have fun and show everyone what we can do!"

"Class 57, Road Hack, Amateur to Ride, may enter the ring," boomed a voice over the speakers.

"Let's go boy, I want to make a good entrance," instructed Heather as she told her horse to trot. Blackjack instantly picked up the trot again and the pair headed towards the in-gate.

The judge, a woman dressed in a pretty blue floral dress, was standing in center ring, looking at the gate. Heather and Blackjack were the second team to enter and as they burst through the entrance, Laura gave a very loud cheer. Heather smiled. She loved showing at Morgan shows where the audience was encouraged to loudly cheer on their favorite riders. Blackjack felt really good; he was certainly enjoying himself. He was moving out at a good pace, although Heather had to hold him back just a bit. He was perhaps a little too eager and his rider wanted to save that energy for the road trot. As they passed the pair that had entered the ring before them, Heather found a good place on the rail and stayed in that position. In order to get the judge's attention, she needed to be near the rail, not out towards the center of the ring. The only concern was cutting across the far end of the ring, near the in-gate, so as not to run into those just entering the ring. As the final entrant came in, the gate was shut and the announcer called the class to order.

"All trot please, all trot," came the command.

With fourteen riders in the ring, Heather would have to be very careful about where she guided her horse. She maintained her position on the rail and continued at the pleasure trot. Up, higher and higher, went Blackjack's legs as he continued to beg for more speed. His neck was up, his head was set perfectly and his ears were forward.   It was a perfect picture of a horse enjoying himself. They made a fantastic pass down the side of the ring and the judge watched them the whole time.   Then the instruction that Blackjack had been waiting for came, "Road trot, all road trot please."

All Heather had to do to get Blackjack to increase his speed was loosen the reins just a tiny bit. Her horse immediately turned on the speed, and without losing his form, began to pass other horses along the rail. Flying around a corner, the horse next to Blackjack got upset and broke into a canter.   Its rider instantly jerked the reins so suddenly that the horse threw his head up, mouth gaping open, in an attempt to escape from the pressure of the bit. That's all Heather saw as they passed by the pair and gained another good position on the rail.

"You're doing great!" encouraged Laura as Heather passed by her. "Ya-ow! Ya-ow!" screamed Laura as she noticed the judge once again looking in Heather's direction.

"All walk," came the next command, much too quickly for Blackjack.

Heather brought her horse back to a walk, but he seemed a bit annoyed at the request. He didn't try to do anything, but he felt a bit too tense. After a brief walk, the command was given to canter, and Blackjack picked up the gait as soon as he was asked.   His canter was a wonderful, smooth, three-beat pace that Heather could sit to all day. After a few times around the ring, riders were asked to increase their speed to a hand-gallop.   Again, Blackjack was extremely eager, perhaps a bit too eager, to turn on the speed. Heather leaned forward slightly, with her hands moving frontward just a little, and off they went. This time, most riders only went around the ring once before the announcer shouted, "Halt!"

All sorts of stops were executed, from quick and smooth to long, drawn out, reluctant slowdowns. Fortunately, this was something that Heather had practiced and Blackjack knew what was expected of him. He stood quietly while the judge slowly looked around the ring. She wanted to see if any of the horses would have trouble standing still, particularly after just running around at the hand-gallop. Out of the corner of her eye, Heather could see one horse pawing and another taking several steps forward. Luckily, Blackjack stood as still as a statue.

"Good boy, easy now," she whispered.

"Reverse and walk on," commanded the announcer.

Relief showed on the faces of many of the exhibitors as the horses were asked once again to move on. The judge slowly turned around, getting a good look at all the competitors. Once satisfied that everyone was doing a flat-footed walk, she asked the ringmaster for a trot. The ringmaster, standing next to the judge and dressed in a bright red hunt coat, signaled to the announcer, who in turn, asked all riders to pleasure trot. All horses, in unison, began to trot.

"Good Heather, keep him right there, he's perfect," encouraged Laura as Heather passed. Heather glanced at her friend and smiled.

"Road trot, all road trot."

Again, Blackjack turned on the speed, although this time, he didn't wait for Heather's cue. As soon as he heard the announcer, he knew he was supposed to go faster and that's just what he did.

"Take it easy boy, not so fast."

But Blackjack wanted to go fast. Heather tightened her reins in an attempt to get her horse to slow down but he resisted. He continued to go a bit too fast and was starting to loose his nice frame. Although he kept his nose in, Blackjack dropped his neck somewhat and began to look slightly strung out. Heather, recognizing that her horse was losing his good body position, tightened her snaffle rein, the upper rein that brings the neck up. Blackjack reluctantly obliged, bringing his neck up and slowing down to a better, more controlled speed. The whole incident lasted less than half a minute and Heather could only hope that the judge had not seen it.

The walk that came between the road trot and canter lasted far too long for Heather. She could feel her horse getting anxious; he was having fun and wanted to run. He certainly didn't want to walk. Heather was relieved when the judge finally asked for a canter and hoped that Blackjack was getting tired. But as soon as the hand-gallop was called, her horse eagerly increased his speed. If he was tired, he certainly wasn't showing it. Twice around the ring and then, "Halt!"

Blackjack immediately came to a dead stop, but like almost every horse in the ring, he chomped at his bit and shook his head a couple of times. He did not want to stand still. After what seemed like an eternity, the judge asked the riders to move out at a walk, but unlike the first time, the competitors were asked to walk on a loose rein.

"Oh, no," whispered Laura to herself, "he's going to loose it."

True to Laura's observation, as soon as Heather loosened the reins, Blackjack began to jig. Heather knew that she couldn't pick up the reins until the judge instructed them to, so she tried to calm her horse with her body. Her legs relaxed, as did her whole body, while she quietly whispered, "Easy Blackjack, it's okay. Relax. Come on, you can do it."

After taking several uneasy steps, Blackjack calmed down ever so slightly. He took painstakingly slow steps, with a brief pause between each movement. He was doing a flat-footed walk, but not a very relaxed one. The judge could certainly mark them down for this poorly executed walk.

"Pick up your reins and line-up!" finally said the announcer.

With a sigh of relief, Heather picked up her reins and asked Blackjack for a trot. She wanted to make one last, brief impression on the judge and she wanted that impression to be of a bold, beautiful road hack horse. Blackjack, thrilled to be asked to move out at a trot, picked up a snappy, high-stepping trot. He carried his neck in a well-arched and proud manner while his head was set perfectly, his ears were pricked forward and he looked eager and happy. The perfect picture. The question was, would it be enough to overcome their little mishap?

The pair, like several other teams, trotted down the rail one last time and then proceeded to the center of the ring where they lined up. Heather found a place near the end of the line and as soon as they were in place, she asked her horse to stretch out in a show pose. First she tapped his left shoulder with her left foot and Blackjack moved his left leg forward. Then, as she was about to tap his right shoulder, Blackjack moved his right leg forward; he knew what he was supposed to do. With both front legs moved forward and perfectly lined up with each other, they looked like champions. A bead of sweat trickled down Heather's face; showing was a lot of work, especially when the judge asked for so much. Her horse was a bit hot too and as they stood there, she could feel his heavy breathing. Glancing towards the far end of the lineup, Heather saw the judge slowly working her way through the group of competitors. Knowing that the judge couldn't see her, she adjusted the back of her show jacket so that it was laid out flat against Blackjack's back. She moved her feet in her stirrups so that her toes pointed forward and each foot was against the inside of the stirrup.

Within a few minutes, it was Heather's turn for a close inspection from the judge. The judge approached, smiled, nodded at the girl and moved slowly around Blackjack. She studied the horse, its bridle and bit, the rider, and how they all fit together to form a team. Once the judge had made her way back to the front of the pair, she asked Heather to back her horse. Heather first tapped Blackjack with her heels to get him to move forward one step because she had learned long ago that asking a horse to back from a stretched position was rather difficult. Blackjack moved forward one step and then, as he felt the pressure on his bit, he obediently took several steps back.

"Thank you," said the judge and she turned her attention to the next rider.

Heather relaxed and glanced over to the rail where Laura was standing. They smiled at each other and Laura gave her friend a thumbs up.

"You may retire your horses," instructed the announcer.

With the judging done, all the competitors made their way towards the in-gate where they were to wait for the placings.

"Hey, that was a great ride!" said Laura, leaning over the fence slightly as Heather approached her section of the rail.

"Yeah, he felt really good. Maybe a little too good; he really wanted to go!"

"I saw that. But it was only a tiny boo-boo. I don't think the judge will pin you down much for it."

"Did she see it?" asked Heather, hopeful that their little blunder might have gone unseen.

"Yup, she sure did."

"We have the results of class 57, Road Hack, Amateur to Ride."

Heather stopped talking. She always got nervous when the results were given.

"First place goes to number 88, 'She's My Gal' ridden by Julie Kenny."

A squeal was heard from a rider. Heather looked to see a girl, about her age, with a huge grin on her face. The rider hugged her big chestnut horse and turned her towards center ring to pick up their ribbon.

"Second place goes to number 92, 'Gallant Image' ridden by Heather Richardson."

"All right Blackjack!" hollered Laura.

Heather smiled, gave Blackjack a big pat on his neck and asked him to trot over to pick up their ribbon. The ringmaster, dressed in his bright red outfit with a wonderful smile on his face, held out a long red ribbon at arm's length. As Heather stopped to pick up the ribbon, she thanked him and he returned the gesture by patting Blackjack and placing the ribbon on his bridle. She then turned her horse back towards the in-gate and trotted out of the ring.

"Not bad, huh?" asked Laura as she ran up to her friend.

"I'm happy. It was a pretty good ride and it was definitely a lot of fun!"

Heather slowed her horse to a walk and dropped the reins as a signal to relax. Knowing that the class was over, Blackjack lowered his head and let his ears flop about as he walked. He looked like a lazy kid's pony, quite a contrast to the bold moving show horse he had been just a few minutes earlier. Laura, having caught up to them, reached over and grabbed the ribbon from Blackjack's bridle so that it wouldn't bother him. Then they all headed towards the barn.

Once Blackjack had been properly cooled down, brushed and put back into his stall with a couple flakes of hay, Laura and Heather headed back to the ring to watch the show. Along the way, they stopped at a food booth and bought a large order of fries, a couple of hamburgers, two large sodas and several chocolate chip cookies. With her class over, Heather found that she was famished and so easily finished a hamburger and her share of fries within minutes. As she began to eat her first cookie, she looked up at Laura who was just about halfway through her hamburger.

"Too bad you're not hungry!" joked Laura.

"I'm not hungry now!" said Heather as she took a big bite out of her cookie, the chocolate chips melting on her hands. "But it's amazing how hungry I get right after a class."

As the friends continued to talk, Heather spotted a blonde haired woman approaching them. She was dressed in a t-shirt and shorts but had her hair pulled back in the typical horseshow bun, and was wearing too much makeup, a sure sign that she had been competing earlier in the day. She was walking up behind Laura with a wide grin on her face. Heather was about to say something but the woman put her finger up to her lips as a signal to keep quiet. Laura, meanwhile, was busy with her hamburger and didn't see Heather smile at the visitor.

"Acck!" squealed Laura, jumping and spilling her soda as this person put her hands around Laura's waist and hollered, much too loudly, "Hey, Laura! How the heck are you?"

Laura turned around to see to whom the voice belonged.

"Oh my gosh! Jennifer, it's so good to see you!" gleefully yelled Laura as she saw who it was. "Heather, this is my friend Jennifer McElroy. We haven't seen each other in what? Five years?"

"Hi, nice to meet you," said Heather.

"Nice to meet you too," replied Jennifer.

"So, how the heck are you?" asked Laura.

"I'm great! And it's so good to see you!"

"Heather, Jennifer and I used to compete against each other all the time when we were kids. Man, that seems like so long ago. Anyway, we'd swap back and forth in the placings all the time and got to be really good friends."

"What are you talking about?" interrupted Jennifer. "You and Rusty were one tough team. I don't think I ever beat you guys. Speaking of which, how is Rusty? Do you still have him?"

"Oh, of course. You don't think Dad would ever part with him, do you? Rusty is nineteen now and retired to a life of leisure. We still trail ride him and Dad drives him a bit, but that's all."

"How's your dad? Still driving your mom crazy with all his silly horse activities?"

"Well, he had to slow down a bit. He had a heart attack not too long ago and had to sell off most of the horses."

"Oh, I didn't know," said Jennifer. "I'm sorry to hear that. It must have really hurt him to have to sell his stock. He worked so long to build up such a great group of broodmares."

"It was hard, but fortunately, his pride and joy, Blackjack, I mean Gallant Image, eventually came home, thanks to Heather here," said Laura as she turned towards Heather, who had stopped eating her cookie to listen to the two friends talk.

"Who is Gallant Image?" asked Jennifer. "I've never heard of him."

"Did you see the road hack class?"

"Yeah, it was a great class. Lots of good horses in there."

"Gallant Image took second."

"Oh, that black horse. He was cool. I really liked him. What's his breeding?"

"His sire is 'Imagine That' who was a world champion. His dam is 'Queen,' one of Dad's old mares."

"I thought Imagine That died really young."

"He did," said Laura, "but he had three foals before he died. Blackjack, that's our horse's barn name, was one of them. Actually, I should really say Heather's horse because she's the one that owns him now, and she was the one riding him in the road hack class."

Heather smiled, not sure of what to say.

"Heather has been a great help at the farm, especially since dad got sick. Now she's just like a member of the family. And you should see her ride!"

"Oh, I did," said Jennifer, "in the road hack class. That was an amazing class and sure required some good riding."

"Thanks, but it was really just Blackjack doing a good job," said Heather, a little embarrassed at the attention she was getting.

Seeing her friend's discomfort, Laura changed the subject.

"Hey, Jennifer, guess what Heather just bought?"

"Hmmm, let me guess... a horse?"

"Yeah," said Heather, feeling more comfortable now that the conversation had shifted away from her riding abilities.

"Tell me all about her, or him. I love hearing about new horses," eagerly said Jennifer as she sat down next to Laura, who was still eating her hamburger.

"Well, I bought her at an auction, which I swore I'd never do but she just looked like she needed a home. She's a Morgan and the best part is," Heather paused to add a little suspense, "the best part is that she is gray!"

"A gray Morgan? That's so cool!" exclaimed Jennifer. But then she stopped, as if trying to remember something. "Oh, wait a minute. It's a mare, right?"

"Yes," said Heather, wondering what Jennifer was thinking.

"Four years old?"

"Yes."

"Really cute and friendly? With a long and fuzzy mane and tail?"

"Yes, that's her."

"I know the horse," concluded Jennifer.

"You do?! Oh, you've got to tell me all about her," pleaded Heather. "We couldn't figure out why anybody would want to sell such a nice Morgan, especially since she's gray and so rare."

"Her name is Tall Pines Shadow, right?" asked Jennifer.

"I don't know. I don't have her papers yet."

"Well, it has to be her. There aren't very many gray Morgans around, are there? I hate to tell you Heather, but the horse was dumped at the auction because her trainer couldn't work with her any more. She belonged to an elderly woman in Maine, really nice lady named Sarah Caine. The horse was sent to a trainer as a three-year-old but never made it into the ring. Unfortunately, Mrs. Caine, who didn't know much about horses or trainers, sent her to probably the worst trainer in New England. Heard the mare was nuts and even threw the trainer. But I suspect the horse was just doing what pretty much any horse would do when stuck for a full year at such a bad place. Anyway, I bet she's pretty much ruined by now. Have you tried riding her yet?"

"Yeah, I just did, yesterday. We had," she paused, "a lot of problems. Who was the trainer?"

"Oh, you've probably never heard of him. A guy named Jim Spencer."

Heather's heart sank and she felt a burning sensation in her chest. The name was one that she had hoped she'd never hear again. Jim

Spencer was a man that considered himself a highly sought after trainer while others considered him a person that didn't know the first thing about horses. His typical training method consisted of taking a horse into training and then, instead of working with the animal to get the best performance, hurting and intimidating it. With terror written on their faces, these horses would storm into a show ring and usually disrupt the class to the point that they would get excused. Then, Mr. Spencer, in a rage of anger, would take his frustrations out on the horse. He was a horrible person who should never have been allowed near horses, as he ruined just about every one he ever touched. Once a horse reached the point of total disobedience, Mr. Spencer would convince the owner to sell the horse cheaply at a local auction and buy another horse. How, Heather wondered, could people be so foolish as to blindly accept what this man told them? Unfortunately, there were many, many unsuspecting owners who simply sent their horses to Mr. Spencer without checking his background and, not knowing anything about horses themselves, took his advice.

Blackjack had fallen into the hands of Mr. Spencer last year, when his new owner got impatient with the first trainer's insistence on taking it slow with the horse. The owner, not wanting to wait to get the horse in the ring, moved Blackjack to Mr. Spencer's barn where the horse was quickly ruined and sent to auction. Fortunately for both Blackjack and Heather, the time spent at Mr. Spencer's had been short and the bond between the horse and the girl so strong, that Heather was able to bring her horse back to a state where he trusted humans. But perhaps if he had stayed in Mr. Spencer's care longer, they might not have had the same good fortune. Since Frosty had been there for a long time, maybe she couldn't be retrained.

"I know him really well," said Heather to Jennifer. "He got his nasty hands on Blackjack for a couple of months and managed to mess him up. Are you sure he trained Frosty?"

"Yeah, sorry. I have a friend that worked briefly, and I mean briefly, at Spencer's and she told me all about the horses there."

"But that doesn't make sense," protested Heather. "If Frosty was there for a whole year, then shouldn't she be a nasty, horrible horse that hates people? Shouldn't she pin her ears back every time I go near her? But she doesn't. She's a sweet, sweet horse who loves attention."

"The reason for that is because Jim Spencer hated the horse. He'd have nothing to do with her in the barn. She was kept in the last stall, down at the end of the barn where Mr. Spencer rarely went. The grooms loved the horse and were always feeding her treats and they're the ones that would get her ready to be ridden. All Mr. Spencer did was get on her in the ring and try to work her. Plus, don't forget that she was raised by Mrs. Caine and spent the first three years of her life with the woman. All Mrs. Caine did was brush and pet Frosty, so Frosty grew up in a very loving home."

"I don't know if I'll ever be able to get Frosty to relax in the ring," sighed Heather. She had suddenly lost her desire to eat and didn't want her last cookie.

The rest of the afternoon dragged by for Heather. They all went to the ring to watch the rest of the day's classes, but while Laura and Jennifer enjoyed themselves immensely, Heather was too upset to have fun. All she kept thinking about was how Mr. Spencer had ruined her horse.

Finally it was time to go home. Laura and Jennifer promised each other to stay in touch and then, giving Heather a hug, Jennifer said her good-byes. Once back at the trailer, Laura began to pack up their gear while Heather gave Blackjack a quick brushing.

"Are you ready?" asked Laura as she lowered the trailer ramp.

"Yup, here we come," replied Heather as she led Blackjack towards the trailer.

As the pair approached the vehicle, Blackjack suddenly stopped, raised his head and took several awkward steps backwards.

"Easy boy, what's that all about?" asked Heather as she patted her horse on his neck. "Did you see that Laura? That's not normal; something is wrong."

"That is really weird, Heather. I don't know what he's doing. Maybe he's just stiff. Walk him around, let me see if he looks lame."

Heather led her horse past the trailer, away from Laura and then back again. Blackjack looked a bit tired but otherwise seemed fine.

"I don't see anything. Let's get him home and see what Dad thinks."

Within a few minutes, the horse was loaded into the trailer, and the group headed towards home. Now Heather had two things to worry about, retraining Frosty and finding out what was wrong with Blackjack.

CHAPTER FIVE

WHAT IS WRONG?

As the trailer pulled into the barnyard, Rusty gave out a loud whinny. In return, Blackjack squealed as loudly as he could. It was his way of saying, 'I'm home!' Chauncy, hearing the commotion from the house, hurried down to the barn. He wanted to hear all about the show, how the class went, if there were lots of good horses competing, what other classes they watched and how those classes went, who was there, either showing or watching and if they had fun. But before he could ask any questions, Heather blurted out, "Something is wrong with Blackjack!"

"What's wrong?" asked Chauncy, the concern in his voice obvious.

"I don't know Dad," answered Laura as she climbed out of the truck. "It's pretty weird. I'm not sure if he's sick or just sore."

"Well, what's he doing?"

"Just as I got on him before my class," replied Heather, "he did this strange backing up thing. I thought he was just being lazy but when he did it again, later in the day, I knew it was something worse. He sort of jerked his head up and took a bunch of steps backwards. Then he just stopped. I walked him around after that and he was fine. Then, when we were loading him into the trailer to come home, he did it again. Since I was leading him and not riding him, I knew he wasn't just being lazy. Besides, he was probably happy to be going home."

"We walked him around, Dad," continued Laura, "but I couldn't find anything. He doesn't look lame."

"Let me see," said Chauncy. "Heather, let's get him unloaded and then walk him around the yard."

While Laura went around to the back of the trailer to let the ramp down, Heather opened the side door and climbed into the trailer. She untied her horse, and then, once the ramp was down and the back bar released, she carefully backed him out. She walked Blackjack around in a couple of large circles and then, at Chauncy's suggestion, walked him in several very small, tight circles, first one way, and then the other. Chauncy kept his eyes on the horse the entire time, studying every little movement. He then had Heather stop and hold Blackjack. With the horse standing still, Chauncy lifted one leg at a time and carefully ran his hands along the bones and muscles of each limb. Then he also checked the hind end, back and shoulders. Finally, he announced, "I can't find anything wrong. He looks fine. Maybe he was stiff from the trailer ride, I don't know. Let's give him a few days off and keep a close eye on him. If the problem comes back, we'll call the vet."

The following day was Sunday, and after spending the morning with her parents at church and then brunch, Heather was dropped off at the barn. She kissed her parents good-bye and ran, as fast as she could, to see Blackjack. She had been unable to think about anything else, and even the problems with Frosty seemed unimportant compared to the strange behavior of her beloved Blackjack. Arriving at his stall, she found him standing in a corner, head down, eyes closed. Thinking there might be something wrong, she immediately entered the stall. Upon hearing the door open, however, Blackjack opened his eyes and came back to life.

"Oh, you were just sleeping," said Heather, relieved that her horse was simply taking a nap.

Grabbing the halter from the door, Heather slid it on Blackjack and led him to the front of the barn where she could groom him. She spent a lot of time brushing him, far more than usual. Having just been at a show, the horse wasn't very dirty, but Heather felt the need to spend some quiet time with him and she truly enjoyed brushing him over and over. Blackjack obviously enjoyed it too as he cocked a back foot to rest it, dropped his head and once again drifted off to sleep. Finally, after about twenty minutes of grooming, Heather decided to take her horse to the ring to let him run and play.

Leading Blackjack out to the ring, Heather saw the horse slowly come back to life. At first his head was down and his eyes looked sleepy, but by the time they had walked the short distance to the ring, Blackjack had raised his head and had a playful sparkle in his eyes. Once the halter was off and he was released, Blackjack squealed, reared, spun around and ran off at full speed to the far end of the ring. There was a spot in one corner that always tended to be a little muddy, particularly in the spring. The horse went right to the area, did a sliding stop that would put any reining horse to shame and then dropped his head down to sniff the ground. Finding the perfect spot, he circled several times, then bent his front knees as he slowly went down. Lying in the mud, Blackjack rolled several times and then just laid there, taking in the wonderful scent of grass that was all around him. He rubbed his neck against the mud, grunted and climbed to his feet. Then he squealed again, kicked up his heels and ran back in the direction of Heather. He looked like he was going to crash into the fence directly in front of his owner, but he quickly turned and continued his fast paced romp. Running along the rail, kicking up his heels and occasionally rolling his neck and head from side to side, Blackjack ran the full length of the ring before he slowed to a trot. Then he broke to a walk, put his head down and discovered that there was plenty of grass in the ring, just waiting to be eaten.

Heather stood at the rail and watched her horse for quite a while. Intent on eating as much grass as possible, Blackjack was oblivious to the attention he was getting. He looked almost comical, covered in mud from his recent roll, and he certainly looked different from the squeaky-clean show horse he had been the previous day. If something was wrong with him, thought Heather, then how could he have run around like a maniac? Surely he'd have just slowly walked to the nearest clump of grass if he wasn't feeling well. Watching from the fence for almost half an hour and seeing no repeat of his bizarre actions at the show, Heather was satisfied that her horse wasn't really sick. He must have just been stiff from riding in the trailer or standing in the stall, as Chauncy had suggested.

As the day began to warm up, the flies came out and started bothering Blackjack. His tail swishing became more and more pronounced as he tried to shoo the pests away. Eventually, they became too annoying and Blackjack gave up his beloved grass for a chance to go into his stall. Heather had gone into the barn to clean stalls and when she came out, she found her horse pacing back and forth near the gate. He wanted to go in. She grabbed his halter, slipped through the rails of the fence and put the halter on her horse. Eager to get in, away from the biting insects, Blackjack tried to push past Heather as she opened the gate.

"Hey," scolded Heather, "stop that! You'll be in your stall in a minute, just be patient."

Blackjack, having been reprimanded, stopped pushing and waited for Heather to walk through the gate first.

Once in the barn, Heather looked at her now dirty horse and decided he needed another brushing. But first she wanted to work Frosty. Putting Blackjack back in his stall, Heather brought Frosty up to the front of the barn for a cleaning. The brushing she received was a much shorter version of the cleaning that Blackjack had been given. Since the horse was going to be worked and probably get hot and sweaty, it didn't make sense to get her super clean. All she needed was to have the dirt removed so that the saddle and bridle wouldn't rub on any debris and irritate her. Within five minutes Heather had her looking pretty good and had even taken out the few pieces of hay in her forelock that had been part of Frosty's breakfast. Like the previous grooming episodes, Frosty seemed to enjoy the attention and certainly didn't seem uptight. But when Heather put the saddle on her, the mare began to fidget. She moved around as much as she could, shook her head several times and, as the girth was tightened, pawed at the ground.

"Come on girl, it is not that bad, really," said Heather, trying to calm the horse. "We're going to do this really slow, okay?"

"You're going to try again, huh?" asked Chauncy as he entered the barn.

"Oh, hi Chauncy. Will you keep an eye on us? We can use all the help we can get!"

"Of course I'll help. There's nothing I like more than working with a horse, even a scared one. Why don't you lunge her first, but instead of lunging in the usual place next to the barn, try doing it in the ring. Let's see if it's the ring that is bothering her, or being ridden in the ring that's the problem."

Putting the lunging halter on Frosty instead of the bridle, Heather led her mare out to the ring. As soon as they were within five feet of the gate, Frosty stopped. Head raised, ears back and feet firmly planted, she made it clear that going through the gate was not something she wanted to do. Heather turned to look at her horse, then at Chauncy, who had been following the pair.

"Go ahead, do what you did the other day. Turn her and back her in," instructed Chauncy.

Heather, now knowing that this little trick was a great way to get her horse into the ring, easily turned the mare, who again thought that she was now being led away from the ring. Instead, she was asked to back and before she knew what had happened, was in the ring. Chauncy shut the gate and leaned against the fence.

"Okay, let's see if she'll lunge in the ring without getting upset," said Chauncy.

Heather let the lunge line out and asked Frosty to move along. The mare, a bit tentative at first, slowly walked a circle around Heather. Her ears kept turning back and forth in an effort to hear every little noise and her head was slightly tilted so that she could see Heather. She looked tense but was not disobedient. As Frosty continued to walk, she slowly relaxed and after about ten minutes was moving out at a brisk walk.

"Trot girl, trot," asked Heather. Having forgotten her lunge whip, she used her free hand in its place. Since she never hit her horses with the whip but only used it to guide them, her arm and hand worked almost as well.

Frosty immediately began to trot. Expecting, once again, that something bad was going to happen, the horse began by trotting much too fast. She went so fast that she broke into a canter for several strides.

"Easy Frosty, not so fast. Easy."

Frosty dropped back into a trot, although it was still much too fast. Her neck was raised, not in a proud arch, but in a tense, straight-up angle. She cocked her head to the side so she could better watch Heather. Knowing that the best response to this nervous horse was to be calm, Heather showed very little reaction. She simply turned as the horse went around her and continued to talk to the mare. Eventually, as Frosty realized that she wasn't going to be hurt, her neck dropped and lost its ugly, tense look. Heather worked the mare on the lungeline for another half an hour. She did lots and lots of walking, mixed with a little bit of trotting. By the end of the session, Frosty looked like an old lesson horse.

"I'd say she has no major problems being lunged in a ring," concluded Chauncy. "She was probably never lunged so she has no reason to fear it. That's good to know but I'm not sure how much help that will be for riding. I think she's got a lot of problems to get over when ridden in the ring. Let's put her bridle on and give her another try. I'll go get it."

Chauncy disappeared into the barn and re-appeared within a minute.

"Here, I'll help you," he said as he assisted Heather in taking the lunging halter off and getting the bridle on.

Frosty quietly stood for the tack change and didn't get upset until Heather got on her. As soon as Frosty felt the weight in the saddle, every muscle in her body got taut and she was ready for a fight. Heather could feel the edginess of the mare and knew that this was not going to be a fun ride. She asked the horse to walk to the rail. Not moving, Frosty immediately flung her head up towards the sky to evade any bit pressure that she thought might be coming her way. Heather squeezed with her legs but still the horse refused to move. The only reaction Heather got was for Frosty to pin her ears back in displeasure.

"Easy girl, I'm not going to hurt you, I just want you to walk to the rail."

Heather clucked and squeezed with her legs but still no response. Finally she used her heels and lightly kicked the mare. Frosty grunted and took a step forward. Heather kicked again and continued to use her voice to try and calm the mare. The second kick seemed to do the job and

Frosty, taking several apprehensive steps in the direction of the rail, finally began to move out. Once at the rail, Frosty broke into a quick paced walk, following the fence line around the ring. The horse continued to throw her head into the air, nose sticking out, in an attempt to get away from whatever was bothering her. The movement of the horse, which was really more of a jig than a walk, was very hard to sit to and gave Heather a stomachache. But she did her best to sit still and not upset the mare further.

Heather worked Frosty for quite a while, but never asked for more than a walk. She had decided that it was more important to get the horse to relax at a walk before moving on to a trot. Unfortunately, Frosty would not settle down. Prancing, jigging, throwing her head up and off to the side, pinning her ears and even stepping sideways were all things that she did. Heather continued to talk to Frosty, and even tried stroking her neck but nothing would calm the horse.

"I think that's enough," declared Chauncy, who had been watching the whole workout. "Why don't you stop now and cool her out. She looks pretty hot."

Heather rode Frosty into the center of the ring and hopped off. She gave the horse several big pats as she verbally praised the mare. With her rider off, Frosty let her head down and began to relax. She was hot and sweaty and had even started to lather up.

"Wow, I can't believe how hot you are, especially since we just walked," said Heather as she loosened the girth and began to lead the horse around the ring.

"I'll be in the barn if you need me," hollered Chauncy as he walked away.

Heather walked Frosty in the ring for quite a while. It didn't take long for the mare to cool off but Heather continued to walk the horse to try and get her used to the ring and not be afraid. It seemed to work as Frosty looked almost sleepy as they walked around and around.

"I bet if I got on you now you'd still go bonkers," sighed Heather.

Remembering that she needed to brush Blackjack again to remove all the dirt he'd acquired while rolling, Heather decided to leave Frosty in the ring by herself for a while. She stopped Frosty next to the closed gate, removed both the saddle and bridle and slipped through the fence. Not sure what her horse would do, she wanted to watch her for a few minutes. Frosty just stood there, looking at Heather.

"What's the matter, girl? Go have some fun!" encouraged Heather.

Frosty stared at Heather for another few seconds and then slowly wandered off to find some grass. Seeing that her horse was content, Heather turned her attention to Blackjack.

When she reached Blackjack's stall, she found her horse laying down, enjoying a brief nap. Not wanting to disturb him, Heather decided that the grooming could wait. But as soon as she started to leave, Blackjack groaned, opened his eyes, stretched his front legs and climbed to his feet.

"Oh, okay, I guess I can brush you now."

Grabbing the halter, Heather opened the door, put the halter on her horse and led him to the grooming area. Blackjack was really dirty, and it never ceased to amaze Heather how fast a horse could get coated in muck. Fortunately, most of the dirt had dried which made it much easier to remove. Unfortunately, as the dirt was brushed away, it gravitated towards Heather and she got it on her clothes, in her eyes, on her teeth and even in her nose.

"Blech," she said as a particularly large clump found its way into her mouth.

It seemed impossible to remove all of the dirt without giving her horse a bath, but when enough was off so that he didn't look dirty, she decided to call it quits. She released the cross ties from either side of Blackjack's halter that held him in place and was about to lead him out for some grass when the horse suddenly jerked his head up. Within an instant he took several uncoordinated steps backwards. Then, just as quickly as the motion had occurred, it stopped. Blackjack seemed startled by what he had just done.

"Chauncy, Chauncy, where are you? He did it again," blurted out Heather.

"I saw it," came a voice from behind Heather.

Chauncy had been coming out of Rusty's stall when Blackjack displayed his odd behavior. Looking at the horse, he said, "I have no idea what he's doing but it certainly isn't normal. I think it's time to call the vet."

****

The following day at school dragged by. It was always a little hard for Heather to get motivated on Mondays but this day was particularly hard. The vet was scheduled to come to the barn at 3PM, which was good because that meant that she could be there when he came. But it also meant that she'd have to wait all day and try to concentrate on her studies. That proved nearly impossible as every imaginable horse disease kept running through her head and she constantly wondered which one her horse had.

Finally, the school day came to an end and Heather bolted to the bus. The ride to Chauncy's was long but uneventful. As the bus squealed to a stop in front of Chauncy's house, Heather anxiously got off and ran to the barn.

"Is he here yet?" she asked as she entered the building.

"No, not yet," replied Chauncy who had Rusty on the cross ties. It looked like the pair had just come back from a buggy ride.

"Has Blackjack been okay?" asked Heather as she walked down to her stallion's stall.

"Actually, I saw him do that same weird backward motion this morning, in his stall."

That wasn't good news, thought Heather. It must mean that whatever the problem was, it was getting worse. She walked into her horse's stall and gave him an apple that had been tucked away in her jacket. As Blackjack slobbered apple goop all over Heather, a truck could be heard approaching.

"He's here," announced Chauncy.

Heather left Blackjack's stall and walked to the entrance of the barn to greet the vet.

"Hey, Chauncy, how are you?" she heard a voice say as she approached.

"Oh, I've managed to stay out of trouble," chuckled Chauncy who had left the barn to meet the vet at his car.

Walking into the barn, the two men almost ran right into Heather. All three stopped just in time to avoid a big crash.

"Whoops!" said Heather. "That was close."

"I guess we all have our minds on other things and are too busy to watch where we're going," joked Chauncy.

"Hi Dr. Reilly," said Heather, holding her hand out.

Dr. Reilly was a very happy looking man, in his mid-forties with a handlebar mustache and a slightly receding hairline. He always dressed in work boots, jeans and a dress shirt. With all the messy work he had to do, Heather could never figure out how he kept those shirts clean, but he did. He also always wore a belt with an enormous buckle that sported a picture of a bucking bronco. It was an award Dr. Reilly was very proud of as he had won it in his college days as a rodeo competitor.

Although Heather had only seen Dr. Reilly a few times, she felt like she knew him quite well. Since the horses had all been healthy for a very long time, the vet had only traveled out to the barn twice a year for shots. But every time he came, he was full of good cheer and had wonderful stories to share about some of the horses he had treated. He was always very glad to spend a little extra time answering questions that came his way. A bonus of these visits was that the horses seemed to enjoy his company. Dr. Reilly had obviously given many, many shots through the years and had perfected his technique so well that the horses usually didn't even flinch. They just nuzzled the vet, looking for treats.

"Hey there, Heather, how are you?" asked the vet, while shaking his young client's hand.

"I could be better, I guess."

"Well, let's take a look at Blackjack and see if we can figure out what the problem is."

The group headed to Blackjack's stall and entered, one at a time.

"Heather, would you put his halter on and hold him, please?" asked Dr. Reilly.

Heather did as she was told and snapping a cotton lead rope to the halter, held her horse in place.

Dr. Reilly took a long, careful look at the horse. "Tell me again, Heather. What has he been doing?"

Although she knew that Chauncy had already told Dr. Reilly everything, Heather didn't want to leave any details out. She carefully explained the bizarre behavior her horse had been exhibiting, repeating much of what Chauncy had said.

"Hmmmm... that does seem strange. Could be any number of things," said the vet, more to himself than anybody else.

Dr. Reilly pulled out a tiny flashlight that he kept in his pocket and aimed the light directly into Blackjack's left eye. Moving the light around the eyeball, the vet leaned towards the horse slightly to get a better view. Then he moved on to the right eye and repeated the test. Turning the flashlight off and putting it away, he took the stethoscope from around his neck, put it on and listened to the horse's heart. First he listened at the chest, then down lower, near the legs, then behind each leg. Finally, he listened at the back. Blackjack, meanwhile, thought that all this attention was great fun and tried to nibble at his lead rope. When Heather reprimanded him, he jumped slightly and distracted the vet.

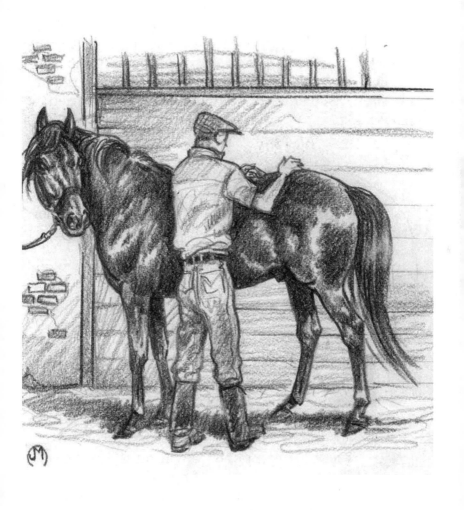

"Blackjack turned towards the doctor..."

"Sorry," said Heather.

But Dr. Reilly was already back at work.

Knowing that he couldn't chew on the lead rope, Blackjack turned towards the doctor, whose back was toward him. Bent over, listening to the heartbeat, Blackjack saw that this human was unaware of his motions. In a quick, playful moment, Blackjack extended his lips and tried to bite the vet on his rear-end.

"Hey, cut that out," scolded the vet as he jumped up.

"Blackjack," said Heather, trying not to giggle. "Shame on you."

But the horse just looked at his owner, trying to figure out what other trouble he could get into.

Finishing up with the stethoscope, Dr. Reilly returned it to its place around his neck and continued his examination by running his hands all along the horse's body.

"What are you doing?" asked Heather.

"I'm looking for any sensitive spots as well as anything that feels abnormal," replied the vet. He ran his hands along the neck, shoulders and legs of Blackjack and then concentrated his energies on the back. Starting from the front and moving towards the tail, he pushed down on the back with enough pressure that his fingertips disappeared into the coat a little. But Blackjack didn't seem to mind; he was too busy moving his lips around, trying to get a good grasp on the lead rope again.

"I can't find anything," announced Dr. Reilly. "Let's take him out and walk him around."

Chauncy was the first to leave the stall, followed by Dr. Reilly and finally by Heather and

Blackjack. They walked out to the yard and waited for Dr. Reilly's instructions.

"Walk him back and forth, Heather. I want to watch him walking away from me and then coming towards me."

Heather led her horse across the large yard and then when she was satisfied that Dr. Reilly had sufficient time to study the horse's movement, she turned and walked Blackjack back towards the vet.

"Do it again," said Dr. Reilly, never even looking up from the horse to Heather.

Again, Heather walked the horse back and forth.

"Now do it at a trot," came the order.

Blackjack seemed a little reluctant to trot and it took several strides to get him going. But once trotting, he decided that it was fun and, seeing that his owner's attention was elsewhere, made a quick grab for the lead rope. Heather snapped the rope and continued to run.

"Can't you stop fooling around and pay attention, Blackjack?" asked Heather.

Heather had to trot her horse back and forth three times before the vet was satisfied. Huffing and puffing, she had no time to catch her breath as she was told to turn him in as tight a circle as possible. Around and around they went.

"Now go in the other direction."

Heather was getting dizzy by the time she was told to stop.

"Well, he seems fine, Heather. I can't see anything wrong. But I'd like to run some blood tests to see if anything abnormal shows up."

Dr. Reilly walked over to his big, red pickup, opened the back door and pulled out a little medical kit. He took a needle and two vials, along with some alcohol and cotton swabs. Cleaning the injection site on the neck with the alcohol, Dr. Reilly inserted the needle into Blackjack's neck. It must not have hurt because Blackjack ignored it while he chewed on the lead rope. He was delighted to have finally been given the chance to chomp on this rope while Heather had decided that chewing on it would keep her horse quiet. The first small vial filled with blood and with lightening speed, Dr. Reilly removed it and attached the second vial to the needle. When that was full, he pulled both the needle and vial out together and walked them over to his truck.

"I'll have the results in a few days," said Dr. Reilly. "Do you want me to call you at home or leave a message with Chauncy?"

"I dunno," said Heather. "I'd like to know as soon as possible but I guess if you leave a message with Chauncy, he's more likely to understand it than my mom or dad."

"Great. I'll have my office call Chauncy as soon as we get the results. In the meantime, don't ride him. I think a little bit of turnout is enough for now."

"Okay."

"Now, who gets the bill?" laughed Dr. Reilly as he pulled out an invoice and began writing.

As Heather took the bill, she knew that the next couple of days would drag by as she waited for the results of Blackjack's blood tests.

CHAPTER SIX

INTO THE WOODS

"Heather, there's some mail for you on the counter," said Mrs. Richardson as her daughter walked into the house.

"Did Chauncy call?" asked Heather as she began to shuffle through some papers, looking for her mail.

"It's right here," said Mrs. Richardson, walking over to the counter and reaching for a large white envelope, "and yes, he did call. He wants you to call him."

"Thanks Mom."

Heather looked at the envelope that her mother had just given her. It was from the Morgan Horse Association and at first Heather was puzzled as to why she was getting mail from them. Then she remembered. It must be Frosty's registration papers! She ripped the envelope open and was thrilled to find a very fancy looking document inside. Taking it out, she saw that is was indeed the registration papers for Frosty. 'Tall Pines Shadow' was written on the top and in the center, a listing of Frosty's ancestors for the last four generations. Flipping the parchment-like paper over, Heather noticed that the previous owner was Sarah Caine, just as Jennifer had said. The most important thing, however, was that the current owner was Heather Richardson. Delighted that she now had proof her mare was a registered Morgan, Heather's first thought was to call Chauncy and tell him about Frosty's registration. Then she suddenly remembered that she had to call him about Blackjack. How could she have forgotten?

Heather's thoughts turned to her black horse and his medical problem. Today was the day the blood test results were due. That's why Chauncy had called. She immediately went to the phone to call him. She was anxious, nervous, excited and afraid, all at the same time. Hopefully, the blood tests on Blackjack showed that nothing was wrong or that he just needed a little rest and would be fine.

"Chauncy?" asked Heather as she heard her mentor's voice.

"Hi, Heather, you got my message, huh?"

"Is the news good?" nervously asked Heather.

"Well, not really. But it's not necessarily bad either. The tests don't show anything conclusive, just that something is wrong."

"What does it say?"

"Hold on, I wrote it all down on a piece of paper. Let me go get it."

There was a loud thunk as Chauncy put the phone down, the sound of feet walking away, and then, a moment later, the sound of feet approaching. Another clunking noise as the phone was picked up, and then, "Here it is. Let's see," a pause as Chauncy looked over his notes, "oh yes, the tests show that Blackjack's hemoglobin is low and so is his hematocrit, but his total protein was quite high."

"I don't understand, Chauncy. Those words are all things that I've never heard of. What does it mean?"

"Basically, according to Dr. Reilly, it shows that Blackjack's immune system is fighting something. What that something is, he doesn't know."

"Is it bad? Can it hurt him?"

"I don't think there is an answer for that right now, Heather. Dr. Reilly said that since Blackjack has a good, healthy coat, is bright eyed, eating well and active, it doesn't appear to be serious. But he wants Blackjack to go on tetracycline for ten days, to see if that will help."

"What's tetra-tetra," Heather stumbled as she tried to repeat the word. "Tetraline?"

"No, it's tetracycline. It's just a common antibiotic. If there is an infection somewhere in Blackjack's body, it should clear it up. We'll get him started on the medicine right away."

"Thanks Chauncy. I really appreciate your help," said Heather. "I'll be down tomorrow."

"Okay, see you then, and try not to worry."

****

Heather was thrilled when the weekend finally came. With the end of the school year fast approaching, homework was abundant as were frequent tests, leading up to finals week. By Saturday, she desperately needed a break from all the schoolwork and intended to spend a good part of the day with her horses.

Blackjack, meanwhile, had been started on his medicine. Fortunately, he did not mind having the tetracycline powder added to his grain. He could always be persuaded to do anything by offering him food, and when given his grain, would suck it up like a vacuum cleaner. He didn't even have time to notice the additional ingredients. Rusty, on the other hand, was a much slower, more careful eater. Anything added to his feed, whether as a supplement or treat, would get a careful inspection before being eaten. Very few of those additions were ever eaten, as Rusty had an uncanny ability to sort out the new ingredients and pick around them, even if they were in powder form. Luckily, it wasn't Rusty that needed the medicine.

When Heather arrived at the barn on Saturday, she first went to Blackjack's stall to visit. It was amazing how well he looked. He was playful, alert, and as usual, hungry. Heather gave him a flake of hay while she just sat in his stall, on the floor, and watched him eat. There was something wonderfully relaxing about just quietly watching a horse eat hay. The smell of the hay, and the gently crunching noises made by the horse, were somehow very soothing.

After Blackjack finished his hay, he wandered over to where Heather was sitting and nuzzled her, looking for more food.

"Silly boy," laughed Heather as she softly pet his face, "can you ever think of anything besides food?"

"Nah, that's all I ever want!"

Heather, who had been sitting against the door, jumped up and turned to see Chauncy standing next to the stall. The quick action startled the horse, who raised his head and immediately saw Chauncy.

"Oh, Chauncy, that wasn't very nice!" scolded Heather.

"I'm sorry, I just couldn't resist."

"Very funny," said Heather, looking at Chauncy with a grin. "Look at how you scared poor Blackjack."

Chauncy looked at the horse, who had already returned to his search for food.

"He doesn't look too upset to me. Looks hungry. Don't you ever feed him?"

"Ha! If I fed him anymore, he'd turn into a blimp!"

The two friends shared a good laugh as Heather walked out of the stall.

Because Blackjack couldn't be ridden, Heather's time would be spent riding Frosty. She had ridden the mare a couple of times during the week, but their progress was non-existent. Each day, the results were the same - a tense, hard ride, followed by a long cooling down period. Frosty was just as nervous as the first day Heather rode her, and Heather didn't know what she could do to get her horse to calm down. The only thing that had changed was that Frosty had figured out every time they approached the in-gate and she was turned around, that she would soon be in the ring. So she was fighting that too. The deception was over.

Today's ride was no different. A struggle just to get in the ring, followed by a very unpleasant ride. Frosty jigged, evaded the bit by throwing her head in the air, stepped sideways and even spun around in a tight circle when she thought Heather was going to kick her. That movement took Heather by surprise and she came very close to falling off. It was a good thing Frosty had such a thick, full mane, as grabbing it was the only thing that kept Heather on the horse. The spin was followed by more jigging, head tossing and pulling at the bit. Frosty even stumbled once because she was so busy tossing her head into the air that she didn't see a small depression in the grass.

"I don't know, Chauncy. I think it's hopeless," said Heather as she rode into the center of the ring after a long, unproductive workout.

"You're doing all the right things," consoled Chauncy as he slipped through the fence and approached. "She may just have too much baggage from her previous training experience to make a good show horse. Maybe we should start to think of something else you could do with her."

"Hey guys, what's up?"

Chauncy and Heather turned to see Laura approaching the ring. She was riding Rusty and the old gelding looked happy to be going out for a ride.

"I didn't know you came home from college this weekend. I thought you had finals coming up," said Heather, who was quite pleased to see her friend.

"I do have finals in a couple of weeks," said Laura, as she rode into the ring and stopped her horse several feet away from Heather and Frosty. "But I needed to get away, have some time to relax before that last, final push. How's Frosty doing?"

"Not much better. In fact, I don't think we've made any progress. She's so incredibly ring-sour that I just can't get through to her," explained Heather.

"She looks pretty hot. How about going for a nice, slow trail ride?" suggested Laura. "That ought to cool her down."

Heather looked at Chauncy to see if he had an opinion.

"Sure, go ahead. It might be the best thing for her. She certainly doesn't like the ring, so maybe she'll be better on the trail."

"Okay, Laura. We'll join you. But it has to be a really slow ride."

"Great. Let's do the 'Loop Ride.' That's always a good, relaxing ride."

The Loop Ride was a three-mile trail that made a big circle and covered some of the prettiest ground in New England. It meandered through sections of forest where the trail was wide and laden with pine needles and then opened up into a huge, grassy field. One section of the trail followed a small brook while another area went up and down several small hills. The final part of the trail went up a long, slowly rising hill that covered almost a quarter of a mile. Heather and Blackjack loved charging up that hill at full speed. But this time there would be no running.

Laura turned Rusty and slowly rode him out of the ring. The pretty bay gelding, eager to get going, broke into a trot and took several steps before Laura pulled him back to a walk. Frosty, not sure what was going on, stood still for a moment, but when Heather asked her to walk forward in the direction of Rusty, she eagerly obliged. As Rusty walked out of the ring, Frosty seemed upset. She too, broke into a trot. Heather, not wanting to further worry the mare, did not pull back on her reins but rather let the horse trot. As they exited the ring and turned a corner, heading away from the barn and to the nearby woods, Frosty quickly caught up to Rusty. Not wanting to stop, she bumped into the gelding's hind quarters.

Rusty, although an extremely well behaved horse, hated having other horses too close and so popped his hind legs up in the air slightly as a threat. It was his way of telling Frosty to back off.

"I wonder if she's ever been ridden with another horse?" asked Heather as she gently tightened the reins to keep Frosty from running into Rusty again.

"I don't know," replied Laura. "But she sure seems to like the idea. Look how she's already clinging to Rusty."

Frosty was, in fact, interested in her companion. Although Rusty had warned her to keep her distance, Frosty wouldn't listen. She came up behind Rusty again and, breaking into a trot, came up alongside the gelding. The two horses were so close that their rumps touched. Annoyed by this action, Rusty pinned his ears back and then lifted his hind leg and kicked out sideways, this time hitting Frosty.

"Hey, cut that out!" hollered Laura as she kicked Rusty in the sides as hard as she could. "You can't do that."

Rusty seemed to get the message and relaxed his ears. Frosty too, seemed to catch on and although she still wanted to be next to Rusty, she kept far enough away so that he couldn't kick her.

"They're just establishing their ground rules," observed Laura. "Once they settle their little fight, they'll be fine."

Frosty seemed a bit nervous but not nearly as much as she had been while in the ring. She jigged and kept trying to break into a trot, but she soon found out that going too fast meant that she would get ahead of Rusty. Rusty, who was moving along at a slow, almost sleepy walk, was now totally uninterested in Frosty. But Frosty did not want to get in front of Rusty; she wanted to be right next to him. By the time they had reached the forest, Frosty had figured out that if she wanted to stay next to her new best friend, she would have to walk.

"Laura, look! She's walking," excitedly said Heather as they entered the forest.

Laura, who had been carefully watching Frosty, was just as excited as Heather.

"That is so cool, Heather!"

"I can't believe that she's finally figured out how to walk," continued Heather.

"You know," said Laura, "I'm not so sure she has figured it out. I think she is pretty unsure of herself and wants to be near Rusty simply because he's another horse. Maybe she thinks it will be safer next to him than out in front. So she's just doing whatever she thinks is necessary to stay close to Rusty. But look at her neck. It still looks really tense."

"Yeah, I can feel the tension but it isn't nearly as bad as it was in the ring."

As they entered the woods, Frosty paused momentarily. With her head still high, she looked around to both her left and right, perhaps to see what dangers might lurk behind the trees. Rusty, who had been on this trail a thousand times, ignored her and kept walking. Frosty, unsure of what to do, decided it best to go back to the barn and started to turn around. Heather turned the mare's head back towards Rusty and squeezed with her legs, trying to urge the horse on. Frosty fought the command, and tried once again to turn towards the barn. Her rider, however, would not let her turn and forced her, by use of the reins and leg pressure, to continue on the trail. Realizing that Rusty was now well ahead of them, Frosty whinnied to her friend and trotted towards him. As soon as she had caught up, she slowed down and tried to nuzzle the gelding. Annoyed that this new horse was still trying to touch him, Rusty raised his back leg in warning and kicked out. His leg did not make contact with Frosty, but it came close enough to send the mare a strong message. She immediately backed off.

Resigned to the fact that they were in the woods, Frosty gave up her efforts to return home and turned her attention to her surroundings. The trail was a wide, meandering path through the forest, with enormous pine trees on either side. Through years of shedding their needles, the trees had created a prickly brown carpet. There were several areas where the sun managed to break through the dense overgrowth and heat up the needles to the point where they gave off a wonderful, heavy aroma of pine resin. The vast quantity of needles also effectively hid the massive root systems of trees that made their way across the trail. Frosty, too busy watching her surroundings at eye level, kept tripping on these hidden roots.

"I think your horse is a klutz!" laughed Laura as Frosty made a particularly clumsy effort to recover from a near fall.

"Nah, she's just too busy looking at other stuff," countered Heather. "She'll be much better once she learns how to cope with trail obstacles."

As the group walked through the woods, Laura and Heather continued to talk. Rusty, a veteran trail horse, was relaxed and knew exactly what to do. Laura kept her reins loose and slipped her feet out of the stirrups. She slowly swung her legs to the rhythm of the horse and let him determine the speed of the ride. Rusty continued on his way with drooping head and flopping ears. Frosty, meanwhile, although not relaxed, was nothing like the horse Heather had just ridden in the ring. She was cautious and alert but not panicked. There was no heavy breathing, no breaking out into a sweat and no lathered coat.

"You know," remarked Heather, "I think Frosty is acting more like a horse who has never been on a trail ride than a horse that is just totally messed up."

"I bet you're right," agreed Laura. "She's nervous, but so is any horse that goes out on the trail for the first time. Knowing Mr. Spencer, he only worked her in a ring so that's what she associates with pain and fear. Ring work, trotting and cantering in a circle, that's where she wants to fight. But trail riding is completely new to her. I don't think she has decided what to do yet. Take it slow and easy and you just might wind up with a nice trail horse."

As Laura finished talking, the horses approached a section of the trail that crossed a small brook. The path went down a tiny incline to meet the water, flattened out for the brook and then rose up again to its original height. The water was only, at its deepest point, about 6 inches deep and the trail was wide and smooth. There were no big rocks or tree roots in the way, only lots of tiny pebbles. Rusty stopped at the water's edge, lowered his head and started to drink. Frosty stopped too but her head was not going to go anywhere near the water. As Rusty quietly drank,

Frosty's eyes bulged, her nostrils flared and she gave out a loud, threatening snort.

"Here we go," sighed Heather. "I knew it was too good to last."

"No, it's okay. I've seen lots of horses freak out at their first water crossing," observed Laura. "Horses don't have very good depth perception so they have trouble figuring out how deep the water is. Of course, they also think there are horse-eating monsters lurking just below the surface. We'll get her to go across the brook; don't worry. It might take a lot of encouragement, but we'll get her to go over."

Rusty raised his head, with water dripping out the sides of his mouth. He grunted and slowly walked through the water and onto the other side of the trail. Thinking that Frosty might decide to jump across, Laura had Rusty take several steps away from the water, leaving plenty of room for the nervous mare to come charging across. Fearing that Rusty was leaving her, Frosty became agitated. She pawed at the ground, snorted again and again and kept trying to turn around. Heather, however, wouldn't let Frosty have her way and forced her in the direction of the water. Using her seat, legs and voice, she urged the mare forward. Laura moved Rusty several more feet away from the brook. Frosty grew still more agitated but no longer wanted to turn around. She wanted to get to Rusty. Standing at the edge of the water, Frosty began to prance in place. Heather could feel the mare's whole body tense up and it felt as if her horse's body was scrunching up underneath her.

"Grab her mane," ordered Laura.

"Huh?"

"Just do it!"

As Heather grabbed a large clump of Frosty's mane, the mare finally got the courage to cross the brook. Terrified of what might be hidden beneath the water, Frosty had no intention of getting one hoof into the mysterious brook. Instead, she scrunched up her body, and using her hind legs to propel her, shot herself up and over. But unlike a good jumping horse who jumps smoothly across, Frosty jumped like an inexperienced, young horse. She jumped much, much higher than she needed to and she jumped from a complete standstill. So rather than being taken effortlessly across, Heather was jarred unexpectedly from the saddle, forced high into the air, and then thrown hard into the saddle on the other side. If she had not been holding onto the clump of mane, Heather would have probably been thrown from the horse. As soon as Heather regained her composure, she lavished huge amounts of praise on her mare.

"Oh, good girl, good girl!" she exclaimed as she leaned over to pet the mare on her neck. "See? That wasn't so bad. Good girl!"

"Now aren't you glad I told you to hold onto her mane?" teased Laura.

"How did you know she'd jump like that?"

"I've seen so many first time trail horses jump a tiny little obstacle like it's a six foot monster. And they all jump the same, much too high and usually from a standstill too. So I had a pretty good feeling of what Frosty would do. I'd say she's a pretty typical horse."

Having her horse called a 'typical horse' was not the sort of thing Heather ever thought she wanted to hear. But today it sounded wonderful. Heather had become increasingly frustrated with

Frosty, wondering why she had ever decided to buy a horse from an auction. Of course there was a reason Frosty was at the sale; nobody could ride her in a ring. What good was she? But now Heather understood. Frosty would probably never make it into a show ring but that was okay. She was a wonderful, sweet, sweet horse and she was going to make a fantastic trail horse. They would have years of fun together, exploring the woods of New England.

Once Frosty had crossed the brook and been given abundant amounts of praise, the friends continued on their way. The trail meandered through several small meadows, went up and down numerous hills and went through some very deeply forested areas. Within this heavily overgrown area there was one point where the trail rounded a sharp corner. The sun, hidden by the enormous trees, made this spot seem unusually dark.

Just as Frosty came around the corner, she spotted a huge white rock, almost as big as she was, right in front of her. She stopped the instant she saw this terrifying object. With bulging eyes, flared nostrils and raised head, she blew through her nose. It sounded as though she was trying to clear something out of her nose. She did it again and then a third time. The girls just laughed.

"Oh Frosty, it's not going to eat you!" giggled Heather.

Being urged on by her rider, and seeing that Rusty was once again getting ahead of her, Frosty reluctantly went forward. But she refused to go anywhere near the rock monster. She continued to blow her nose at it as she passed, ever so carefully, along the far side of the trail. She was so close to the trees that her side rubbed up against one.

"Hey, move over!" commanded Heather as she forced Frosty to get back onto the trail. Heather had to raise her leg up and towards the center of her saddle to avoid being hurt by the tree. Unfortunately, her saddle wasn't as lucky and as Frosty continued, it was forced against the tree. There was a dull, rubbing noise as the leather saddle flap scratched against the bark. As soon as they were past the tree, the trail opened up slightly and Frosty was able to stay comfortably away from the big, white horse-eating monster. Once the rock was behind them, Frosty relaxed and Heather let her leg down. Looking at her saddle, the damage was obvious. There was a big scratch along the side flap, right where Heather's leg had been.

"Oh shoot Frosty. Why'd you have to do that??? This is my good saddle; it's my only saddle! Now look at it!"

"Let's see," said Laura who had turned Rusty around so she could get a better look. "Hmmm... Well, it doesn't look too bad. Your leg will cover it up when you show. Just consider it the price of teaching your horse to be a good trail mount."

"That's easy for you to say!" said Heather, feeling only a little bit better. "But I saved up for six months to buy this saddle."

"When we get home we'll see if we can rub the mark out with leather polish. It won't be that bad, I promise. Now come on, let's get going."

The ride continued for another half hour. The trail, which was a big loop, circled around and crossed the brook once again. This time the crossing was in a pasture and Frosty had plenty of room to maneuver herself. She paused, pranced in place and still needed lots of encouragement but was not nearly as frightened of the water as before.

She still, however, insisted on jumping over the obstacle and once again took a huge, awkward leap. This time, though, Heather was prepared. She had a big clump of mane clutched in her hand and knew what to expect. She easily stayed in the saddle although the hard, sudden landing still jarred her bones.

The rest of the ride was an easy walk back home. Upon their arrival, both riders dismounted right outside the barn. After letting Rusty and Laura enter, Heather led Frosty to the cross ties. Laura led Rusty partway down the aisle, then let go of the reins and slapped Rusty gently on the rear. The pretty bay gelding, as reliable as ever, simply walked into his stall and waited for his saddle and bridle to be taken off.

Heather took Frosty's bridle off and, while leaving the reins around her neck, slipped the mare's halter on. Then she removed the reins and handed the bridle to Laura who put it in the tack room.

"She was great, wasn't she?" Heather remarked as she took Frosty's saddle off.

"Yeah, I think you should be really, really happy," replied Laura. "It's pretty obvious now that Frosty's problems are all centered around working in a ring. I've seen a couple of other horses that were like that, and they never did get over it. But they both found other things that they were good at. One made a fantastic driving horse and the other was a competitive trail horse."

"Well, there, how'd it go?" asked Chauncy as he walked into the barn.

"It went really well!" exclaimed Heather.

As Heather brushed Frosty, she told Chauncy all about their ride. Looking back on her experience, the crazy jump over the brook now seemed funny and even the brush with the tree didn't seem too bad. As she finished her story, Rusty poked his head out of his stall, the door still open.

"Whoops," said Laura as she ran towards Rusty, "I think I forgot somebody!"

While Laura tended to Rusty, Heather put her brushes away and led Frosty back to her stall.

"You're such a good girl," said Heather as she offered Frosty a peppermint. "I'm so proud of you."

Frosty took the treat with her lips, slipped it into her mouth and then threw her head up and down several times as she chomped on the hard candy. Spitting a little bit of it out as she chomped, she was soon looking for more.

"No, that's enough for now. Its time for me to brush Blackjack."

Heather turned her attention to her big black horse. As she led him towards the cross ties, she thought about the medicine he was taking and if it was working. It seemed to her that his weird backing up motions were becoming more frequent, which shouldn't be the case if the medicine was effective. But she wasn't sure if the increasing frequency was simply because she was more aware of the problem or maybe because she now perceived every little movement as being related to his problem.

As Heather began brushing Blackjack, the horse grabbed one of the cross ties with his mouth, as was his habit, and began to chew on it. He loved to shake the chain hard so that it made loud clunking noises as it hit the wall. Up and down, back and forth, went his head. He was certainly having fun. Blackjack wasn't very dirty so Heather was using her softest brush, one that didn't clean well but felt good to the horses. As she moved towards the back of the horse and began brushing his rump, Blackjack began to quiver. He stopped playing with the cross ties and just stood like a statue. As Heather continued to brush, Blackjack continued to shake. The shaking was restricted to the back of the horse, in the general area where Heather was brushing. The girl noticed her horse's reaction immediately and stopped brushing. As soon as she stopped, so too, did the shaking. Heather took a step back and looked at her horse. Blackjack had turned his head so he could get a better view of what was going on near his rump. His ears were forward and he didn't seem to be in pain. Rather, he seemed confused.

Heather decided to try brushing again, to see what Blackjack's reaction would be. She brushed his rump and again, he began to quiver. Moving down one leg, the bizarre motion of the horse continued. Heather stopped brushing. The quivering stopped. She moved to the other side of her horse and brushed his rump. Her horse began to quiver again. The reaction was the same as she brushed down the leg. Continuing along the side of the horse, the motion stopped and Blackjack relaxed. Returning for a moment to the hind end, the shaking started as soon as the brush rubbed the horse's body.

"Chauncy, we need to call the vet. Blackjack is getting worse!"

CHAPTER SEVEN

THE MYSTERY GROWS

"Is this an emergency?" asked the scratchy, cranky voice over the phone.

"I don't know. I'm not sure how serious it is," replied Heather, hesitantly.

"Well, Dr. Reilly is out of town for the weekend so unless this is an emergency, you'll have to wait until Monday. If it is urgent, then we will call Dr. Kemp, the vet that is listed as Dr. Reilly's backup for the weekend. But of course, you'll have to pay extra for him to come out on a Sunday."

"I guess it can wait until Monday. I'd really like Dr. Reilly to come out and look at my horse, not another vet."

"Okay then, give me your name and phone number and I'll have Dr. Reilly's office call you first thing Monday."

Heather gave the woman her name but then explained that Dr. Reilly would have to call the home of Chauncy Campbell to set up the appointment since she would be in school. Hanging up the phone, she turned to Mrs. Campbell, who had been standing next to her during the call.

"She wasn't very nice," said Heather.

"Oh honey, don't take it personally. On the weekends, when his office is closed, Dr. Reilly switches his phones over to an answering service. That lady you called works for the answering service. She answers calls for lots and lots of different people and companies. She probably talks to dozens of people each hour, and I bet a lot of them aren't very nice to her. So I guess she's just cranky at the world, not you."

Like her husband, Mrs. Campbell always knew what to say to make Heather feel better. With her soft-spoken manner, short, gray hair and constant smile, Mrs. Campbell was the sort of person who everyone wanted as a grandmother. She always wore pretty dresses over her slightly plump body and was normally busy in the kitchen cooking up something wonderful. Although not into horses like her husband and daughter, she had accepted the fact that her family was deeply involved with the animals and had learned to put up with them.

With the exception of their youngest child, Laura, the Campbell's rarely saw their own children. Laura's four siblings had moved far away and so Mrs. Campbell was happy to have almost daily visits from Heather. On the weekends, when Heather would spend a good chunk of the day riding her horses, Mrs. Campbell would always have a sandwich waiting for the girl around noon. If Heather didn't make her way up to the house for lunch, Mrs. Campbell would stroll down to the barn and practically drag the youngster back to the house, all the while explaining the importance of a proper lunch.

"Chauncy went to the feed store to get some grain and my mom is going to be here at any moment, so I'll be gone when he gets back. In case he's not here tomorrow when I come to ride, will you let him know that Dr. Reilly will be calling Monday morning?"

"Oh sure, dear. No problem. Don't worry, I'm sure Blackjack will be fine," said Mrs. Campbell as she gave Heather a great, big bear hug.

Just then a car horn beeped.

"That's Mom! Gotta run. Thanks so much, Mrs. Campbell," said Heather as she dashed out the door.

****

Monday morning found Heather in her American History class taking a surprise quiz. How on earth could she focus on the problems that led up to the Civil War when she knew that Chauncy would be talking to Dr. Reilly about Blackjack at about the same time? She knew that Blackjack was getting worse and was incredibly anxious to hear what Dr. Reilly would have to say. When Heather had gone to the barn on Sunday, Blackjack had done his weird backing up maneuver a couple of times, including once while eating in his stall. Then, while on the cross ties, he again began to quiver when the brush touched him near his rump. But it was quickly getting worse. Instead of just quivering, his back legs shook so much that it seemed he would fall down. In fact, as they shook, Blackjack's rump collapsed slightly so that he almost looked as though he were sitting down. Whatever was making her horse sick had to be discovered soon, before Blackjack had to suffer too much.

After school, Heather rode the bus directly to Chauncy's house. She was restless and worried about what Dr. Reilly had said. Did he find anything? Would he decide to change the medicine? What was causing Blackjack's problem?

"What did the vet say?" asked Heather as she walked in the barn and saw Chauncy sweeping the aisle.

"What? Oh, hi Heather. I didn't see you," replied Chauncy, looking up, away from the floor. "Dr. Reilly hasn't come yet."

"He wasn't here today?" Heather asked, surprise in her voice.

"No, sorry. He was going to come out early this afternoon but then he got an emergency call."

"Isn't this an emergency call?"

"Actually, no. Dr. Reilly says that as long as Blackjack is eating well and seems active, he's okay. He thinks this is more of a long-term problem. Besides, his emergency was a mare that was having problems foaling. That's not exactly something that can wait."

"I guess you're right," said Heather. "But I'm really worried about my horse."

"I know you are, but we have to try not to worry. It won't do any good you know. Worrying will only get you more upset and Blackjack will pick up on that."

"When will Dr. Reilly be here?"

"He said he'd try to come today if it wasn't too late. It all depends on how long his emergency call takes. If it is too late, then he'll come out tomorrow."

"Oh," was all that Heather said.

Disappointed that there was not yet an answer for Blackjack's problem, Heather turned her attention to her horse. His head was leaning out of the stall and he was watching his owner with great interest.

"Hi, boy. How are you today?"

In reply, Blackjack shook his head up and down. It was one of his ways of asking for a treat.

"You think I have something good for you, don't you? Oh, all right. Here's a peppermint," said Heather as she reached in her pocket and pulled out a little red and white mint for her friend.

Blackjack eagerly took the treat and continued to shake his head up and down as he crunched the mint. In just a few moments, the treat was gone and the horse was looking for a second.

"That's enough, silly. You can't spend your whole day eating."

Heather haltered her horse and brought him up to the cross ties for grooming. She was careful to only use her softest brush on Blackjack and barely touched him as she brushed his back legs and rump. But again, whenever she would brush in those areas, the horse would quiver terribly. The shaking was definitely getting worse as the horse's hind end almost collapsed with just the slightest touch. Not wanting her horse to be subjected to more discomfort, Heather discontinued her grooming and led Blackjack outside.

The spring grass was growing and the ground was covered with a deep, dark green blanket. Blackjack, eager to get some of this grass for himself, pulled at the lead rope. Heather found herself being dragged by the big, black horse towards the nearest clump of grass. Normally, she would never have put up with such behavior but because her horse was sick, she was willing to overlook his loss of manners. As soon as they reached the grass, the pulling stopped as

Blackjack's head shot to the ground and his lips began pulling at the blades of green. As the horse continued eating at a frantic rate, it was hard to believe that he was sick. His coat glistened, his eyes were bright and he seemed content.

After about fifteen minutes of grazing, Heather decided to bring Blackjack back into the barn. She knew that eating a lot of lush spring grass, with all its sugars and other tasty ingredients, was like eating candy for a person. A horse could easily get sick by eating too much. Blackjack, however, insisted that he needed to eat more. He was reluctant to leave the tasty grass and Heather had to really pull hard on the lead rope to get his attention. As they walked toward the barn, Blackjack took every opportunity to drop his head and grab a clump of grass. Walking near the barn, the horse, eager for one last bite of grass, pulled at an especially thick and juicy looking cluster of green goodies. Instead of getting lots of grass, however, Blackjack retrieved just a few blades and lots of roots and dirt. By the time they entered the barn, the grass had been eaten and the stallion's lips reached the dirt. He shook the mass of dirt and roots in disgust and dropped it on the floor.

As soon as Blackjack was safely returned to his stall, Heather turned her attention to his stable mates. Laura wouldn't be back from college until next weekend, after all her exams were done. Because Heather did not feel Frosty was ready to go out on the trail without Rusty's guidance, she decided to wait to ride Frosty until Laura returned. In the meantime, Heather would lunge her gray mare and turn her out in the ring. Frosty's mandatory quarantine had ended on Sunday and she had been moved into the stall next to Rusty. The two horses had spent part of Sunday sniffing noses between the walls of their stalls and sticking their heads out of the doors, looking at each other. There had been some squealing, a little kicking at the wall and lots of pinned ears as the two neighbors became acquainted. But within half an hour, the commotion had died down. Rusty had lost interest and Frosty had decided that kicking the wall didn't get her any closer to her friend. All had been quiet since then. Now, thought Heather, it was time to turn them out together and see what they would do.

Rusty was led out to the ring first. Heather knew that he'd be unlikely to stand at the gate, which would make it easy for her to bring another horse into the ring. She was right. As soon as he was in the ring, Rusty turned his attention to the grass that had sprung up in the center and wandered off to eat his fill. When Frosty was led out to the ring, she whinnied and pranced. Fortunately, going into the ring to graze was different to Frosty than being taken in with a bridle and saddle, ready to work. Seeing her friend Rusty, the pretty mare was extremely anxious to get near him and she crowded around Heather as the girl opened the gate. As soon as they entered, Frosty tried to run off and therefore made it difficult for Heather to take her halter off. But once it was off, the mare went running towards Rusty. The old gelding, who had been quietly eating, seemed annoyed at this sudden intrusion. He was not in the mood to play. Raising his head and pinning his ears back, Rusty was giving the young mare a clear sign that he wanted to be left alone. But Frosty ignored the signals and crashed into the gelding, in an eager attempt to get close to the horse. Rusty swung his hind end around towards the mare, kicked out and squealed. In response, Frosty reared up and struck out with her front legs. Rusty kicked out again and then trotted away. Frosty, thinking it was a game, followed the gelding and continued to annoy him. Rusty kept trying to eat but was constantly interrupted by the mare, who wanted to nuzzle and get acquainted. A little more squealing, kicking and rearing and then the two horses settled down.

Rusty was clearly in charge and led the way. Wherever he went, Frosty followed, never allowing more than five feet to separate them. This closeness obviously bothered Rusty who had never enjoyed the close companionship of another animal. He seemed to prefer people and would always keep his distance from other horses. But Frosty wouldn't allow him to get away. She insisted on being near him and after a while, Rusty seemed to accept the fact that the annoying little mare would not leave. If he wanted to eat, he'd have to ignore her and that's just what he did.

As the horses settled down, Heather leaned against the gate and watched the peaceful scene. Her mind started to wander back to Blackjack until she heard a truck approaching. She turned and saw Dr. Reilly's big, red pickup pull into the driveway.

"Hi there, Heather," greeted Dr. Reilly as he got out of his truck.

"Hi Dr. Reilly. I didn't think you were going to make it today."

"Neither did I. But my last patient, the mare that was foaling, apparently decided she didn't want me to help her and managed to foal right before I got there. She had a beautiful spotted baby."

"An Appaloosa?" asked Heather.

"Yup. I think the owner is going to call the foal 'Spot'."

"That's a, um, er, cute name," laughed Heather, thinking the name rather silly.

"So how's our boy today?" asked Dr. Reilly, as he and Heather walked into the barn.

"He's getting worse," replied Heather. "I don't think the medicine is working. He's still doing his weird backing up thing and then, when I brush him, even with a really soft brush he gets upset."

"What do you mean by upset?" asked the vet.

"Whenever I brush his hind end, it starts to quiver. It started as just a little shake, but got worse and worse. Now he almost collapses when I brush him there. Let me show you."

Heather brought Blackjack to the front of the barn, attached the cross ties and began to brush.

"See? He's okay when I brush his front like this, and even his sides. Now watch."

Heather moved to the back of Blackjack and began to softly brush her horse. As she did, the horse, as if on cue, began to quiver and his hind end dropped so much that it seemed he might collapse. Dr. Reilly carefully watched the horse, standing off to the side. When Heather had finished her little demonstration, Dr. Reilly walked to the back of the horse and began to press his hands against the horse's body. Just as he did when brushed, Blackjack shook and started to drop his hind end towards the floor.

"I don't know, Heather. This is very strange."

"Could it be EPM?" asked Chauncy who had walked into the barn as Dr. Reilly was examining Blackjack.

"No, no. I don't think so," answered the vet. "EPM is usually rather one-sided but this behavior is very evenly distributed between the two sides."

"What's EPM?" asked Heather, not wanting to be left out of the conversation.

"EPM stands for Equine Protozoal Myeloencephalitis," explained Dr. Reilly.

"Equine Proto what?"

"That's why it is referred to as EPM," said the vet, smiling. "It's a lot easier to say. EPM is a neurological condition caused by a tiny little parasite. It is transmitted to a horse via an intermediate host such as a raccoon or opossum and can cause a whole series of different neurological problems. Symptoms can include gait abnormalities, general weakness and muscle wasting but it is usually asymmetric, which means one-sided. I really don't think that's what we're dealing with here. I'd like to do some tests to rule out other conditions."

"What do you need to do?"

"Blackjack won't even notice, Heather. I need to take some more blood samples. I want to test for Lyme Disease, which he could have picked up from a tick. It's a simple blood test and we can let Blackjack chew on his lead rope while I do it, okay?"

"Sure," replied Heather, trying to smile.

Dr. Reilly left the barn to get some supplies from his truck. He returned a few minutes letter with a couple of vials and needles. As suggested, Blackjack was allowed to chew on his lead rope while the quick procedure was performed.

"Heather, I've also taken a sample so that I can do an onsite glucose test. It will only take a couple of minutes to get the results. I'll be right back," explained Dr. Reilly as he once again left the barn. As promised, he returned in just a few minutes.

"Okay, just one more blood test, I promise," said the doctor. "Blackjack's glucose level is slightly elevated so I want to test his insulin level. One more test, okay boy?" asked the vet as he gave Blackjack a pat. Blackjack ignored him as he continued to chew his rope.

Glucose, insulin, Lyme Disease. All these strange terms being tossed around made Heather's head spin. What did it mean? What was wrong with her horse?

"Great," said Dr. Reilly as he finished extracting blood from the neck of the horse. "All set."

"What is the insulin test for?" asked Chauncy.

"I want to rule out Cushing's Disease," came the answer.

"Cushing's?" exclaimed Chauncy. "How could he have Cushing's? He's too young for that! Cushing's is a disease of old, arthritic horses!"

"Typically, yes," agreed the vet. "Unfortunately, there are instances of much younger horses having Cushing's."

"What's Cushing's Disease?" interrupted Heather.

"Cushing's Disease is caused by a tumor of the pituitary gland. It can't be cured but it can be managed with medication."

"Oh," was all Heather could say.

"But don't horses with Cushing's," continued Chauncy, "have thick, wavy coats that they can't shed out, even in the summer? Look at Blackjack! He's got a sleek, shiny, beautiful coat."

"Yes, he does. But the disease doesn't always manifest itself with those symptoms. Let's not get ahead of ourselves. Let's wait and see what the tests reveal, okay?" asked the vet, looking at Heather.

Heather looked upset as she replied, "all right."

"Don't worry Heather," consoled the doctor. "We'll get this figured out. It should take three or four days to hear back from the lab and I'll make sure that my assistant calls me, even if I'm on the road, as soon as the results are faxed to her. I'll call as soon as I hear."

****

The rest of the week dragged by as Heather anxiously awaited the test results. Each day she would rush to the barn after school and head straight for Blackjack's stall. He was still taking the medicine that Dr. Reilly had prescribed after his first visit but it was having no effect, at least none that Heather could see. Blackjack still exhibited the strange backing up movements and his hind end sensitivities seemed to be getting worse.

Frosty, on the other hand, was doing quite well. Because Heather wanted to wait until Laura returned from college before she rode the mare out on the trail again, Frosty was getting a little vacation. Each day she was turned out into the ring with Rusty. Eager to play with her friend, Frosty would prance and pull at the lead rope in an attempt to get to the ring as soon as possible.

Rusty, reluctant at first to put up with this new annoyance, seemed to finally accept the pesky mare. In fact, Rusty seemed to be getting rather fond of Frosty. He had been spotted grazing so closely to the gray mare that their muzzles touched. The amazing thing was that Rusty didn't kick, squeal or even flatten his ears. He now seemed content to have this new companion. Frosty's persistence had paid off.

The week progressed slowly but without incidence. Blackjack still looked sleek and happy, with a good appetite, and only those who watched him closely could tell that something was wrong. Frosty and Rusty continued to play and get better acquainted. Finally Friday came and Heather rushed to the farm.

"I heard from the vet," said Chauncy to Heather as she entered the barn.

"What did he say?" anxiously asked Heather.

"Well, there's good news and then there's, well, not so good news. The good news is that the test for Lyme Disease came back negative. So Blackjack doesn't have Lyme. That's really good."

"Okay, but what's the bad news?"

"It really isn't that bad," said Chauncy, trying to diminish the impact of his previous words. "The insulin test that Dr. Reilly did showed that Blackjack's insulin level is quite high, well above normal."

Heather suddenly felt ill.

"What does that mean?" she asked, her voice barely audible.

"It could mean a couple of things," explained the old farmer. "According to Dr. Reilly, Blackjack could have Cushing's Disease, he could be insulin resistant or it might even be something else."

119

"Cushing's?" mumbled Heather, dreading the diagnosis. "Will he die?"

"Oh, no, honey," answered Chauncy, putting his arm around his young friend. "There are medications available for horses with Cushing's. It can't be cured, it will never go away and you'll have to carefully monitor his food and exercise. But it can be managed. We're going to take Blackjack off the tetracycline that he's been taking and put him on a new medicine. It's called cyproheptadine. It is a medication used for horses that have Cushing's. If Cushing's is the problem, then according to Dr. Reilly, we should see improvements in Blackjack pretty quickly."

Heather felt very guilty for the way she was feeling, but she wasn't sure she wanted Blackjack to get better after taking this new medicine. She hoped there would be an easier, better diagnosis. If he did improve, then it would mean her horse had Cushing's Disease, a chronic problem. Heather had read a magazine article that told her a horse with Cushing's would never get better and might actually, over time, slowly get worse. Did Blackjack really have Cushing's Disease? Did he have a neurological problem like EPM? Something even worse than Cushing's? What was wrong with Blackjack?

CHAPTER EIGHT

PLANNING A TRIP

Dr. Reilly had said that improvements in Blackjack's condition should be seen quickly with the new medication, if he was, in fact, suffering from Cushing's Disease.

"You should see a change within about a week," explained the doctor's assistant when Heather had called. The worried girl, eager to know how soon her horse's weird behavior would stop, had made the call in the hopes of getting some reassurance from Dr. Reilly. "Hopefully, Blackjack's coordination problems will start to lessen within a few days and disappear completely in about a week."

After a week had passed and no improvement was seen, Heather contacted Dr. Reilly to see what she should do. It was decided that Blackjack should stay on the medication for at least another week.

Because Blackjack could not be ridden, Heather had turned her attention almost entirely to Frosty. She still lavished lots of love on Blackjack, but after grooming him and turning him out in the ring each day, there was very little else she could do. With Laura back from college for the summer, the two friends were able to go riding every day. Heather wanted to take full advantage of the training opportunities that riding with Rusty gave her, so each day, rain or shine, she went straight to the farm after school.

Heather, seeing that Frosty was much more relaxed out on the trail than in the ring, had decided that Frosty would be a trail horse. Ring work became a thing of the past as every ride was ridden along the wonderful trails near Chauncy's farm.

By the end of the second week, Frosty was relying less and less on Rusty for security and more and more on Heather. There was no doubt that Frosty was a cautious mare who required lots of encouragement, but she was also a very gentle and trusting horse who was willing to let another guide her. At first that somebody was Rusty, but as Frosty relaxed and Heather grew more confident, the mare stopped clinging so tightly to Rusty's side and was even willing to fall back behind the old gelding without getting upset.

Another positive sign of Frosty's improvement was that she was no longer returning from each ride drenched in sweat. She had not been asked to do anything more than a simple, relaxed walk each day, and soon, she came to realize that there was nothing that would hurt her. She had a wonderful, ground-covering stride that frequently forced Rusty to trot, just to keep up. The mare, however, was still a bit awkward when it came to obstacles such as the stream that crossed the trail. She needed far less encouragement to cross the water, although, without Rusty crossing first, she would always refuse. But as long as her friend was on the other side, Frosty would go across. She still, however, had not refined her jumping style and Heather was forced to cling to the saddle each time as her horse jumped high up into the air to avoid the water.

On a particularly nice spring day, as the two friends rode their horses along the usual trail, they became lost in conversation. The horses were relaxed, with heads lowered, ears flopping and tails swatting at the occasional fly. As the group approached the final part of the trail, the section that went up a long, slowly rising hill, Laura looked at Heather and smiled.

"What? What do you want?" asked Heather quizzically.

"Oh, come on, let's do it," replied Laura, with a bit of a devilish smile on her face.

"Do what?"

"Don't you think your mare is ready? She's doing so well."

"Ready for what?" asked Heather, more perplexed than ever.

"Ready for a good, fun trot up this hill."

"I don't know Laura. She's been going so well, I don't want to push her."

"I think she's ready. I'll go first with Rusty and you can just follow. Try to push her into a trot. If she won't go, or gets really upset, I'll stop. Come on, it'll be fun."

"Okay, we'll give it a shot."

With that, Laura tightened her reins slightly and clucked to Rusty. The old gelding was off in an instant. Heather repeated Laura's actions, and to her surprise, Frosty immediately broke into a trot. Her head rose high into the air, and Heather felt the mare's body tense a bit, but the young horse did not fight. Heather kept her reins somewhat loose, hoping that the lack of tension in the reins would help relax the mare. Frosty, seeing Rusty get further and further away, wanted to catch up to him and it only took a few seconds for her to do so. The trail was rather wide at this point and it easily allowed the horses to trot side-by-side. As Frosty challenged Rusty's lead, the gelding increased his speed. To keep up, Frosty began to trot faster. Faster and faster they went, each horse egging the other on. Both horses had their ears pricked forward, eager to keep going. Heather, who had never experienced a relaxed trot on Frosty, was amazed to find that it was so smooth. It was as if they were floating on air. Frosty's legs extended well in front of her as she raced to the top of the hill, still far away. Before long, the mare had increased her speed to the point where she was doing an extremely fast extended trot, far too fast for Rusty. The gelding, much to his dismay, slowly fell behind. But that didn't make Frosty hesitate for a moment. Instead, she increased her speed even more. As they climbed the gently rising hill, the mare's body and head lowered to the ground a bit. Her legs were digging into the soil to help move her along, and she was using her entire body in much the same way as a racehorse. Heather, too, changed her body position. She leaned forward and down, moved her hands along the mare's neck and lowered her head so that Frosty's long mane flew into her face. The two were now acting in unison, with the rhythm of Frosty's quick movements flowing perfectly with Heather's position. The sensation was fabulous; Heather felt as though she were flying.

Finally, the top of the hill was in sight. Heather raised her body as a signal to her horse to slow down. At first Frosty didn't respond so Heather tightened the reins slightly and used her voice to ask for less speed. The mare, starting to feel a bit tired from the energetic run, obediently dropped her speed and broke down to a walk. As Rusty caught up, panting in delight, Heather looked over at Laura.

"Wow! That was incredible! Did you see us, Laura? Did you see how fast Frosty can trot?!"

"My gosh, I don't believe it!" exclaimed Laura. "Frosty has the most amazing extended trot. It's so fast but it's also so beautiful. It looked like you two were floating. Poor Rusty got left in the dust!"

"Her trot is really smooth too," continued Heather. "She didn't seem to get upset either, the way she always did in the ring."

"No, I don't think she was even thinking of her past ring training. She just wanted to race with Rusty." Laura paused and then continued, "Hey, Heather, I just had an idea."

"Oh, oh. I'm afraid to ask," said Heather, not too sure what to think.

"Remember Jennifer? My friend who you met at the horse show?"

Heather nodded.

"She called me a couple of nights ago to invite me on a three-day ride."

Heather looked interested.

"Jennifer says she's been going for several years and that it's really fun. The ride is held in Vermont and she says that over fifty people go each year. Jennifer is trying to get a big group of friends to come along and I said I'd go. Would you like to come?"

"Me? I don't know. I've never been on an overnight ride. What's it like?"

"It is so much fun! You get to ride all day and then camp out at night. I've gone on a couple of different rides and had a blast."

"Do you think Frosty and I could do it?" asked Heather.

"With that trot? Geeze, you'd be out in front of everybody else. You sure wouldn't have any trouble keeping up. Besides, it's a pretty easy ride. Everybody goes at their own pace and the idea is to have fun, not cover a lot of miles."

"When is the ride?"

"Next month. What do you say, you wanna come?"

"Sure, it sounds like a great way to enjoy my horse. I'll ask my parents about it tonight."

Just as Heather agreed to go on the ride, they approached the barn. Blackjack, having been put out in the ring before the girls had left on their ride, whinnied a greeting. Frosty and Rusty both looked at the black horse, but neither of them made a sound. They were ridden to the barn where, having already cooled off, they received a good brushing and were then put back in their stalls. Heather gave each horse a flake of hay while Laura put the bridles and saddles away. Then Heather went out to the ring and brought Blackjack into the barn. As she threw a flake of hay into his stall, she noticed something.

Blackjack, bright eyed and as hungry as ever, was contentedly munching his hay. But there was something different about him, something that Heather couldn't quite put her finger on. His back, that was it, his back looked strange. Blackjack's backbone seemed to be sticking out slightly. How was that possible? 'What a strange thing,' thought Heather. Too strange, in fact, to really be true. She must be imagining it. She looked at Blackjack's face, those big, soft eyes, his sleek, healthy coat and great appetite and decided that it was nothing. 'Heather, you're always worrying about your horse,' she thought, 'and now here I am making up problems in my mind. There was nothing wrong with Blackjack, the medicine was working.'

****

"Chauncy, come quick!" hollered Heather.

It was Saturday morning, just a few days after Heather had noticed Blackjack's backbone sticking up above the rest of his back. Heather had come to the barn early to feed the horses and go for a ride with Frosty.

"What's wrong?" asked Chauncy.

"Look at Blackjack's back!" said Heather, panic in her voice.

Chauncy peered into the stallion's stall and saw what was worrying Heather. Blackjack's spine was indeed sticking up, or rather, his back had dropped away from the spine. The bone was plainly visible which was odd, given the fact that the horse was fat and sleek. No ribs could be seen as they were all covered with a healthy layer of fat and muscle. Only the backbone was affected.

"I've never seen anything like this," Chauncy mumbled to himself as he entered Blackjack's stall for a closer look.

Chauncy carefully examined the horse, felt his back, and pressed down on each side to see what sort of reaction he might get. Blackjack flinched, but he kept eating as Chauncy pressed harder on his back.

127

"I don't know what this is," finally concluded Chauncy. "I think we better call the vet."

When Dr. Reilly arrived, he was equally puzzled by Blackjack's new symptom.

"I hate to admit it, Heather, but I'm stumped," admitted Dr. Reilly after he had carefully examined Blackjack. "This combination of symptoms is very unusual. I thought we were dealing with Cushing's, but now...now, I'm not so sure. I'd like to have Dr. Hutchinson come take a look at Blackjack."

"Dr. Hutchinson?" asked Heather. "Who is he?"

"Dr. Hutchinson is another vet, one who specializes in internal medicine. He's very good at discovering what's beneath all sorts of problems. I think if we work together on solving this puzzle, we might just be able to figure it out. I'll call him right away."

The following day, a tan pickup truck pulled into the driveway at Gallant Morgans. A short, chubby man with black hair and a well-trimmed beard stepped out of the truck and headed toward the barn where he was met by Heather, Laura and Chauncy.

"Hi there, I'm Dr. Hutchinson," he said as he shook Chauncy's hand.

"Nice to meet you, Dr. Hutchinson," replied Chauncy. "I'm Chauncy Campbell, this is my daughter Laura and this worried looking young lady is Heather."

"Laura, Heather, nice to meet you both," said Dr. Hutchinson as he shook both their hands. "Heather, Dr. Reilly and I had a long talk about your horse and he's faxed me copies of all the lab reports. From the blood work, I can tell you that your horse is mildly anemic with an elevated insulin level. But I suppose you know that already, so I think it's time to take a look at Blackjack to see if we can figure out what is causing these symptoms."

Heather led Dr. Hutchinson to Blackjack's stall and prepared her horse for yet another examination. With his halter on and a stranger in his stall, along with his owner, Blackjack knew that he was once again the center of attention. Unlike the previous examinations, however, this one took much longer. Dr. Hutchinson spent close to an hour examining the black horse, laying his hands on the horse's back, legs, neck and ears. The veterinarian also carefully examined the horse's eyes and nostrils. What surprised Heather, however, was the extensive amount of time spent listening to Blackjack breathing. Dr. Hutchinson placed his stethoscope on the horse's chest, several areas of the neck as well as numerous points along the back, and quietly listened to the calm in-and-out breathing of the horse. He spent close to twenty minutes just listening and during this time, Heather became acutely aware of her own breathing. Blackjack, meanwhile, was getting bored and tried to entertain himself by chewing on his halter rope. Heather quietly tried to stop him, but the more she reprimanded him, the more annoyed he became. By the time Dr. Hutchinson was finished, Blackjack was restless.

"I think he's had enough of this," said Dr. Hutchinson. "Heather, would you please lead him outside. I'd like to see how he moves."

Heather did as asked and, once outside the barn, walked Blackjack away from and towards the vet several times.

"Now do it at a trot," instructed the veterinarian.

Heather once again led her horse back and forth several times.

"Okay, that's enough," said the doctor. "Bring him over here."

Heather walked Blackjack over to Dr. Hutchinson so he could once again examine the horse. The horse, noticed Heather, was breathing heavily.

"Gosh, Blackjack," said Heather, "I'm the one who should be out of breath, not you. I guess all that time off is catching up with you."

"That's an interesting point," commented Dr. Hutchinson. "Even if he isn't being worked, your horse should not be panting at all. But look at him! It's as if you've just taken him for a canter across a field."

Dr. Hutchinson was right; Blackjack was panting as if he'd just gone for a short run. How could that be?

"Why is he so out of shape?" asked Heather.

"I don't think that is what's causing his heavy breathing," noted the veterinarian. "I'm sure you noticed how much time I spent listening to him breath earlier. The reason for that was because I was very surprised to find that his breathing was quite shallow."

"Does Cushing's do that?" asked Laura, who had been watching from behind the vet.

"No, this doesn't appear to be Cushing's."

Heather was instantly relieved but also perplexed.

"But what about the medicine he's been taking? It's for Cushing's Disease and it was working."

"I believe," explained Dr. Hutchinson, "that it was just a coincidence. I don't think the medicine had any real effect."

"But if it isn't Cushing's," she asked, "then what is it?"

"I can't be sure, but I think what we're dealing with is a chronic infection of some sort. Maybe an abscess in the lungs or abdominal cavity."

"That would cause all those weird symptoms?" asked Heather.

"Yes, it could. And it would certainly cause very shallow, labored breathing. He may appear to be happy and comfortable, but I believe Blackjack is in a fair amount of discomfort. His outward appearance is a testament to his tough Morgan character. He's really quite miserable."

"What can we do?" asked Heather, her concern apparent.

"Well, even though he's not feeling well, I think the best course of action is to give him a little time to see if this infection will clear up on it's own. We'll give him some different antibiotics to help him along and take another blood test in a month. I'd like to see a natural resolution to this problem, if possible. But, if the infection is still present in a month, then you'll have to bring him in to Dr. Reilly's clinic for further testing. However, that can get rather expensive so let's try to resolve this without going that route."

"What sort of testing would you have to do? Would you have to do surgery?"

"Oh no, Heather, nothing like that. We might do an endoscopic and tracheal wash and culture or maybe take some x-rays to see if we can find the source of the infection. It won't hurt him, I promise."

Relieved that Blackjack would not have to undergo any painful tests, as well as the fact that he didn't have Cushing's Disease, Heather happily took the medicine that Dr. Hutchinson gave her.

"What about his other medicine, the stuff I was giving him for Cushing's?" asked the girl.

"Oh, don't give him that anymore. You only want to give him the antibiotics that I just gave you."

****

The following month flew by as Heather was kept busy caring for her two horses. Blackjack was doing as well as could be expected. Although he didn't appear to be getting better, he seemed to have stabilized. The awkward backing motion had completely disappeared and although his back still looked horrible, with his spine protruding above his back muscles, the condition had not gotten any worse. He continued to eat like a vacuum, sucking in everything he was given in record time and his coat still glistened in the sun. Heather was so relieved to learn that her horse didn't have Cushing's and couldn't wait to have his final blood test taken. She was sure the results would show that his infection, if that was indeed what it was, would be gone.

Meanwhile, Heather prepared Frosty for their first three-day adventure. The little gray mare was going great, becoming more confident with each passing day. The pair usually rode with Rusty and Laura, but occasionally, when Laura couldn't make it, Heather still rode Frosty through the wooded trails. The Morgan wasn't quite as bold when faced with obstacles without Rusty to guide her, but she did her best. There was no panic in her actions, just a bit of reluctance to go forward. She would sniff, snort and paw as she investigated the scary looking water, rock, or tree, but with a little encouragement from her rider, she eventually found the courage to face the obstacle.

Finally, the much-anticipated date arrived. It was time to load the horses into the trailer and head up to Vermont for their three-day ride. Everything was packed in the truck and the girls were eager to get going. Dr. Hutchinson had returned a few days earlier to take Blackjack's final blood test and promised to have the results upon their return. Heather couldn't wait to spend three wonderful days with Frosty as they explored the woods of Vermont.

"Almost ready?" asked Laura as she loaded Rusty into the trailer.

"Yup," replied Heather, leading Frosty towards the trailer.

Frosty, sensing the excitement, knew that something special was going on. She insisted on lowering her head and smelling the ramp before getting on the vehicle, just in case there was some new odor that she needed to know about.

"Come on, Frosty, let's go," encouraged Heather.

Frosty, her nose touching the ramp, snorted and then raised her head. She looked around her, saw Rusty already tied inside and whinnied. Heather, meanwhile, pulled gently on the lead rope to encourage the mare to get on the trailer. Seeing that her owner wanted her inside the strange stall, the mare obediently walked onto the trailer. Frosty then patiently waited as Heather tied her lead rope to the trailer. As soon as her young owner was out of the way, the hungry mare turned her attention to the overflowing hay bag in front of her. Rusty was already totally fixated on his hay bag, eating as though he hadn't had a meal in days. Heather exited the trailer through the side door and then slipped around to the back to help Laura raise the ramp.

"Are we ready?" asked Heather, unable to contain her excitement.

"Let's just do one final check," suggested Laura as she walked over to the truck and peered into the back. Heather climbed into the bed of the truck to get a better look. "Grain and hay?" asked Laura.

"Check," said Heather as she located the items.

"First Aid kit?"

"Check."

"Rain gear, food for us, water, and hardhats?"

"Check, check, check and, wait a minute," a pause, and then, "oh, here they are. Check. All here."

"Two saddles with girths and blankets, bridles and brushes?"

"Yup, all here."

"What about our cell phones?"

"I put them in the glove compartment," answered Heather.

"Better double check that."

Heather climbed out of the back of the truck, climbed into the front and found the cell phones.

"They're both here."

"Great, then let's get started!" ordered Laura, now showing as much excitement as Heather.

Laura climbed into the driver's seat, turned the ignition on and slowly drove the truck out of the driveway.

"Heather, Heather! Telephone!" bellowed Mrs. Campbell's voice from the house.

Laura immediately stopped the truck and both girls looked in the direction of the house. Heather jumped out of the truck and hollered back, "Can you take a message?"

"Hold on, dear," came the reply.

Heather looked at Laura, shrugged her shoulders and waited. After a few moments, Heather decided to run up to the house. As she approached, Mrs. Campbell came running out.

"Oh, there you are, Heather."

"Who was it, Mrs. Campbell?"

"It was Dr. Hutchinson, calling with the results from Blackjack's blood test."

"That was quick," said Heather. "What did he say? Is Blackjack all better?"

"Unfortunately, dear, there is no improvement. Everything is still the same."

Heather felt a pit grow in her stomach.

"Dr. Hutchinson called?" asked Laura who had followed Heather to the house.

"What did he say?" asked Chauncy, who had heard the commotion from the barn and followed the girls to see what was up.

"According to the doctor," responded Mrs. Campbell, "there's been no change in Blackjack's condition. He wants Heather to bring her horse to Dr. Reilly's clinic on Monday morning for testing. He's already talked to Dr. Reilly and they will both be there to work together on Blackjack. I told him that we'd have the horse there first thing on Monday. Hope that's okay."

"Sure, I can truck him over," replied Laura. "The clinic isn't very far from here. Besides, it would be interesting to see how they x-ray such a big animal." Turning towards her friend, Laura continued, "Hey, Heather, don't worry. Between Dr. Reilly and Dr. Hutchinson, there's no doubt that this mystery will get figured out. Blackjack will be okay."

"I shouldn't go on the ride; I need to stay home with Blackjack," was all Heather could say.

"That's crazy," scolded Chauncy. "Why should you stay home? Blackjack will be fine. I'll keep an eye on him, give him lots of attention and as many peppermints as he wants. There's nothing you can do here; you'd just be hanging around wishing you were on the ride with Laura. Go have some fun!"

Heather looked at all her friends, each one smiling at her, encouraging her to go enjoy the ride. They were right, she thought, what could she do if she stayed home?

"Okay, I'll go. But Chauncy, you have to promise to give Blackjack lots of love while we're gone!"

"Don't worry kiddo. Now go have some fun!"

CHAPTER NINE

A NEW CONFIDENCE

The trip up to Vermont was uneventful. Heather was quiet as her thoughts were on Blackjack and not on the excitement of the impending trail ride. Laura, meanwhile, had tried to start up a conversation with Heather, but had failed. Every time Laura asked a question, Heather answered with a single word - yes, no or maybe. Deciding that it wasn't much fun having a one-way conversation, Laura finally gave up and most of the trip was spent in silence.

The long ride was mostly driven on the highway. As they got closer to their destination, the small hills gradually changed into mountains. Then the mountains slowly seemed to get higher and higher. The green of the trees seemed to change too, getting darker and darker, making everything look so lush and thick. After a few hours, Laura pulled off the highway and drove slowly through a quaint little village. The main street seemed practically deserted, with just a few cars and nobody walking along the sidewalks. Driving through the village, the next turn was onto a somewhat bumpy, poorly paved road. The road went up and down and around far too many corners. They passed by several streams that followed the road, or was it, thought Heather, the same stream that kept disappearing and then reappearing several miles away?

In most areas, there were very few houses along the road. Occasionally, there would be a cluster of several houses, a church or some other official looking building, and then nothing again for several miles. It certainly was beautiful, thought Heather, but why would people want to live here, so far away from civilization?

Finally, after what seemed like hours, the truck turned off the main road and onto a small dirt road. There were so many ditches and bumps that Laura was forced to drive slowly to avoid tossing the horses around in the trailer. They followed the road for about a mile and then turned off into a big, grassy field. The truck, now going even slower, cautiously made its way to the center of the field where lots of trucks and trailers had already parked. Tossing its occupants around as it traveled over all sorts of bumps, ruts and dips in the field, their truck made its way past several rows of vehicles until it finally came to a vacant spot.

"I guess we can park here," said Laura, mostly to herself as she turned the ignition off.

"Wow, there are a lot of people here," noted Heather as she slowly came back to life.

"Yeah, there should be a good crowd today. Jennifer said this has become a really popular ride. Now," continued Laura, "let's check on the horses and then go get signed in."

The friends climbed out of the truck and peered into the trailer to see how Rusty and Frosty had handled the ride. As the side door to the trailer opened, the two horses looked over to see who was opening the door. Seeing that it was just Heather and Laura, the horses immediately turned their attention back to their half empty hay nets.

"Guess they're more interested in food than in us," laughed Heather.

"Come on, they're fine. Let's go check in," suggested Laura.

Heather gently closed the trailer door and then quickly proceeded, with Laura, to the far end of the field where a couple of large, portable tables had been set up. As they walked through the tall grass, Heather noticed that her shoes and pant legs were getting damp. The late morning sun had been fighting clouds all morning and was just starting to win the battle. As the sun got stronger and stronger, it was drying up the remnants of the early morning dew, but not fast enough to keep Heather's shoes dry.

"Oh, man, I hate wet shoes," she complained as they approached the tables. Shaking the dew off her pants as best she could, Heather turned her attention to the registration process. There were three lines of people waiting patiently as three volunteers, a man and two women, sitting at the tables, did their best to get everyone signed in quickly.

"This line looks the shortest," said Heather as she approached the middle line.

Heather and Laura waited quietly until it was their turn to register.

"Hi and welcome to the Mountain View Trail Ride!" greeted the woman sitting behind the table. The volunteer was a burly, older woman with long brunette hair pulled back into a ponytail. It looked strange to see a ponytail on someone over fifty, thought Heather, but then again, it gave the woman a very friendly appearance. "Can I have your names?" asked the volunteer.

"I'm Laura Campbell and this is Heather Richardson."

The volunteer looked down at her numerous papers, shuffled them for a moment until she found the information she was looking for. "Found it," she said to herself as she pulled a paper to the front of the pile. "Laura, I have you listed as riding a horse named Frosty. Right?"

"No, actually I'm riding Rusty. Heather is riding Frosty."

"Oh, hmm... that's strange," mumbled the volunteer. Then, after a moment, "No problem, we can fix that."

The woman picked up her pen, drew arrows from the horses' names to the correct rider and then looked up and smiled.

"Oh, I see that Heather is a minor. Laura? Are you her guardian on this ride?"

"Yes, I am. I'm over eighteen." "Great. That makes it much easier. Now, all I need to see are your Coggins tests."

Laura reached into her back pocket and pulled out two yellow sheets of paper. They were official documents from the veterinarian that showed their horses had had a blood test to prove they were free from the virus that causes Equine Infectious Anemia, a contagious and sometimes fatal disease. The woman took the papers, carefully checked them, matching horse and owner names, verified the dates and handed the papers back to Laura.

"Looks like you're all set," said the woman as she reached behind her chair to a large cardboard box. Pulling out two large envelopes, she said,

"Here, these are your information packets. They have a map, safety tips, tickets to today's lunch and Sunday evening's barbecue. Lunch is at noon, over in that far corner. After lunch there will be a short meeting to go over the ride and then everyone will set out at their own pace. Oh," she continued as she handed the girls their packets, "there's also a little gift in each envelope. Enjoy."

"Thanks!" replied Heather and Laura in unison.

The friends turned back towards their trailer and as they wandered across the field, opened the envelopes.

"Oh cool!" exclaimed Heather as she ripped open her envelope. "Look!"

Heather reached into her envelope and pulled out a light blue baseball cap. The cap had the words 'Mountain View Trail Ride' embroidered in green on the front along with a mountain landscape. Heather plopped it on her head.

Looking into her envelope, Laura smiled when she saw an identical cap. "That's really nice of them," she said.

Reaching the truck and trailer, Laura lowered the ramp and let the horses out one by one as Heather got a bale of hay from the truck and, tossing it out to the ground, broke it open. She then took the hay nets from which the horses had been eating, refilled them and tied them to the outside of the trailer, one on each side. By the time she was finished, Laura had both horses also tied to the outside of the trailer, one on each side. Next, they each filled a water bucket from a large, five-gallon jug that they had brought from home. Drinking eagerly, Rusty took his fill of water and then rubbed his head on Laura's leg while Frosty pawed the ground.   She could hear Rusty splashing the water in his bucket with his nose and saw Heather still busily getting her water. Frosty wanted her water and she didn't like to wait.

"Oh be patient," scolded Heather. "I'm going as fast as I can."

Heather poured the water into the bucket as fast as she could, spilling quite a bit as she did. Then lugging it over to her horse, she lifted it up to Frosty's nose so the horse could drink.   Frosty eagerly consumed most of the water, pausing only once to look up at Heather.   Finally, having had her fill, the mare lifted her head and, like Rusty, began to rub it on Heather.   Unlike Rusty, however, Frosty's mouth was still full of water which she dribbled out all over Heather's leg.

"Oh, gross, Frosty. Did you have to?" asked Heather.   Although she didn't really like getting wet, Heather wasn't angry with her horse. She knew that Frosty was just playing and so she thought it was funny. Giving her horse a gentle pat, she put the bucket aside and went to find her grooming kit.

The next half hour was spent pampering the horses. Grooming them until there wasn't a speck of dust left on their hides, picking the debris out of their hooves, combing out their manes and tails and getting every single knot out, and giving them several peppermint treats kept the horses happy. They were certainly enjoying their time tied to the trailer. Eventually, a voice was heard yelling,

"Lunch, lunch is served!"

All the participants made their way to a third table that had been set up a short distance away from the registration tables. Several people were busily putting out stacks of food, taken from boxes behind the table. As Heather and Laura approached the line, they heard a voice behind them call out,

"Hey, Laura, you made it! I'm so glad! This is going to be a blast!"

Heather and Laura turned in unison to see Jennifer running up to them.

"I was wondering when I'd see you," said Laura, hugging her old friend. "What horse did you bring?"

"Oh, I brought Robin. She used to be my show horse but I retired her from showing a few years ago. Now she's my trail buddy."

"Is she a Morgan?" asked Heather.

"Yup," answered Jennifer. "A pretty bay mare, mostly Lippitt breeding."

From her long talks with Chauncy, Heather knew that Lippitt was a Morgan bloodline that came from the hills of Vermont.

"She sounds nice," said Heather. "I can't wait to meet her."

The friends talked up a storm as they waited in line. It had only been a few weeks since Laura and Jennifer had talked on the phone, but they wanted to know everything that had happened to each other during that time. As Heather approached the front of the line, she handed a young man her lunch ticket and in turn was given a sandwich, tightly wrapped in cellophane.

"It's peanut butter and jelly," he said as Heather looked at it quizzically. "There are also chips and brownies further down the table, if you'd like."

"Thanks," said Heather, taking the sandwich and turning her attention to the variety of chips thrown onto the table. Grabbing a bag of sour cream chips and a brownie, again wrapped in cellophane, Heather made her way to the end of the table where there was a big metal trash barrel, filled with ice and soda cans. Picking out a root beer, Heather wandered over to a flat piece of ground, away from the commotion and sat down. Laura and Jennifer followed, still talking non-stop. Several friends of Jennifer joined the small group and lunch passed quickly as everybody got acquainted. Before long, a middle-aged, bearded gentleman with a pudgy stomach got up in front of everyone and began to talk.

"May I have your attention?" he bellowed in an effort to stop all the talking. "Can everybody hear me?"

Several people answered, "Yes!" all in unison.

"Good, then we can get started. First, my name is Tom Finnery. I'm the President of the Mountain View Riding Club and I'd like to welcome you all here today for our eighth annual ride. I'd like to go over some of our rules before we get started..."

Mr. Finnery continued to talk for a while, covering even the most basic of trail riding topics. Towards the end of his safety speech, some of the girls in Jennifer's group, having heard the same talk several times, grew bored and began to whisper amongst themselves. They giggled, threw grass at each other and generally ignored the speaker. Heather thought this was rude and tried her best to listen to Mr. Finnery. Finally, the talk ended as everybody was instructed to get their sleeping gear and anything else they might want taken to the evening's campsite and load it into one of three trucks waiting near the group.

Immediately, over fifty people stood up and headed to their trucks to get their gear.

Once all the assorted gear had been tagged and carefully placed in the transportation vehicles, everyone turned their attention to their horses. Whinnies and snorts were coming from all directions as the animals all felt the excitement building in the air. Frosty seemed anxious as Heather put her saddle and bridle on. The gray mare refused to stand still and instead kept moving back and forth, back and forth, as much as her lead rope would allow.

"Frosty, stop that!" scolded Heather in a voice that got her horse's attention.

Frosty momentarily stood still for Heather, but then she let out a loud whinny. Rusty responded with a call of his own. Then the anxious mare began to paw the ground. She wanted to go!

Heather finally got her horse tacked up and waited for Laura. Laura, meanwhile, had been busy closing up the trailer and locking the truck. Everything had to be secure as they would not return to their trailers until the end of the ride. Then, with great speed, Laura got her horse ready. Grabbing her hardhat from the hood of the truck, Laura put the hat on and mounted her horse. Heather did the same.

"Do you have your cell phone?" asked Laura.

"Yup, right here in my saddle bag next to my water bottle," answered Heather as she tapped her small carrying case. Heather's mom had bought both girls a small saddlebag that attached to the front of their saddles. It allowed them each to bring water and a few munchies along on their long ride. Chauncy, meanwhile, had bought each horse a new bridle, ones that, with a couple of simple snaps, converted into halters. These thoughtful gifts would certainly make things easier during the ride.

The first group of horses had already headed out when Heather, Laura, Jennifer and several other young women gathered near the entrance to the field. They would have to ride down the dirt road that they have driven in on but in the other direction, for about half a mile before finding the trail. The horses were all impatient; few were standing still. Some pawed, others walked around in tight circles while still others kept taking a step or two forward followed by another step back at their rider's command. The horses were as excited as their owners. Frosty, having never been on a ride with so many different horses, was particularly nervous. She refused to stand still and instead insisted on walking around to meet her new friends. As Heather tried to hold her in place, Frosty stretched out her nose towards the nearest horse, a big, chestnut mare. The mare, noticing Frosty's interest, turned towards her and the two animals touched noses. The big mare immediately let out a loud squeal as she struck out with her front leg. Frosty, shocked at this response, jumped back. Her quick movement startled the horse standing next to her. This horse, a bright bay thoroughbred, turned his tail towards Frosty and raised one hind leg in a threatening manner. The riders of these horses, busy talking to long lost friends, were not paying close attention to their horses and didn't seem worried about the ruckus. Heather, however, seeing that her mare was upsetting some of the other animals, asked Frosty to walk away from the commotion. Frosty obeyed, but it wasn't long before she began inching her way towards another horse, this time a smaller, bay mare, the one that Jennifer was riding. This horse, Robin, was not at all interested in talking to Frosty and completely ignored her. Jennifer, noticing the interest Frosty was displaying, told Heather that Robin had been on so many trail rides she no longer got excited when she met new horses. As the group waited for the last two riders to join them, Robin's eyes began to glaze over and her head slump. She was falling asleep. Standing next to the very sleepy horse seemed to have a calming effect on Frosty, who slowly began to relax.

"Frosty will be fine, Heather," explained Jennifer. "All horses tend to get excited on their first ride. But once she gets going, she'll be having too much fun to be nervous." Then, turning her attention to the group, Jennifer shouted, "Hey, is everybody that's coming with my group ready?"

The other riders, twelve in total, hollered back their desire to get going and so, the group set out on the ride.

Heading down the bumpy dirt road, the horses slowly drifted apart as their riders broke up into smaller groups of two or three. Jennifer, Laura and Heather led the pack, and Frosty, happy to be next to Rusty, relaxed and, with her far reaching stride, was soon leading the group. Heather had to frequently stop her mare so that Rusty and Robin could catch up and, as Frosty began to get ahead again, found herself repeatedly looking back to participate in the conversation.

By the time the riders reached the trail entrance, Heather's neck was starting to get sore from having to turn backwards so often.

Meanwhile, other riders, having the same problem as Heather, passed them. Jennifer and Laura, oblivious to their slow pace, had started talking about horse shows from their childhood. Rusty and Robin were content to be going slow and it wasn't long before they were at the back of the group. Frosty, however, was not interested in going at such a sluggish pace.

"Hey guys," interrupted Heather, "I'm going to catch up to the others. Frosty wants to get going."

"Sure, go ahead," replied Laura. "We'll be in the back here if you need anything."

Heather happily asked her horse to move out and Frosty eagerly obliged. She broke into a swift, flat-footed walk that would put the best endurance horse to shame. The trail was a wonderful meandering path that led through a huge pine forest. There was a heavy blanket of pine needles on the ground and the scent of pine filled the air. The sounds of horses snorting and of their hooves hitting the hard summer earth were easily heard. Heather quickly caught up to two riders, one riding a pretty black Morgan mare and the other on a lovely chestnut Arabian. Both girls appeared to be about the same age as Heather.

"Mind if I join you?" asked Heather as she approached from the back.

"Sure, come on, we love company!" greeted the girl on the Morgan. "My name is Holly and this is Sarah."

The three girls exchanged greetings. Holly was a pretty young woman with shoulder length black hair, a bright smile and sparkling eyes. Her hair was perfectly combed and she sported a tiny bit of make-up, just enough to accentuate her lovely hazel eyes. She wore a light blue polo shirt with a white band around the collar and, unlike almost everybody else on the ride, her clothes appeared spotless; there were no dirt stains or signs of horse slobber anywhere. In contrast, her companion Sarah looked like a tomboy. Her hair was pulled back in a single ponytail with strands of hair flying loose from every possible part of her head. Her riding helmet was bright purple and held on with a tattered looking safety harness, and her t-shirt looked like it had seen better days too. But like Holly, she had a very pleasant smile.

"What are your horses' names?" asked Heather.

"My horse is named Polly," said Sarah, "and Holly's horse is called HotShot."

"That's a funny name," laughed Heather.

"Well," explained Holly, "her real name is Adel's Queen of Hearts but she just loves to show off so we call her HotShot. The name really fits, trust me."

All three girls broke out in laughter at once. Frosty, meanwhile, was eager to meet the new horses. As the new friends talked, Frosty walked up to Polly and sniffed her side. Polly, in return, let out an annoyed squeal as she raised her hind leg in warning.

"Sorry about that," said Sarah, turning her attention to her horse. "It usually takes her a little while to warm up to a new horse."

"No, it's my fault," apologized Heather. "I shouldn't have let Frosty just walk up to your horse like that. This is her first ride and she's still getting used to all the excitement."

"Don't worry about it," advised Holly. "She'll get used to it quickly. Look, she's already decided that introductions are over and it's time to move on."

Frosty had, indeed, decided to stop sniffing the new horse and had turned her attention back to the trail. She was still eager to move at a quick pace and so, continued her fast walk. It was a pleasant surprise for Heather to find that these two horses, Polly and HotShot, were also fast and their speed was closely matched by Frosty. Frosty, happy not to be held back, settled down and the three horses contentedly explored the trail with their riders.

The time spent in the saddle flew by as Heather and her new friends talked non-stop, all the while enjoying the beautiful Vermont scenery. The trail didn't vary much from beginning to end, with a widely cleared path that was expertly marked with bright yellow ties. There were several stream crossings and a couple of footbridges through somewhat muddy areas that needed to be carefully maneuvered around, but otherwise, the trail was unchallenging.

Occasionally, others from their group would meet them, usually at a stream crossing. Everybody would stop their horses to let them drink and rest. As the horses relaxed, people would start talking and laughing. It was like a big party and Heather loved it. Once all the horses had had their fill of water, the group would slowly set out on the trail again. Within a short period of time, they would once again have drifted into their little groups.

It was at one of these water crossings that Heather got her first glimpse of Frosty's emerging self-confidence. The stream was very wide at this crossing, perhaps fifteen feet from side to side. In the past, Frosty would cautiously walk to the edge of the water and slowly put her head down to drink. But this time was different. Perhaps she was overly thirsty, or the bugs were starting to bother her. Whatever the reason, Frosty boldly stormed into the water and was soon up to her knees in the cool, refreshing liquid. Heather, surprised at this action, nonetheless encouraged it and gave her mare several pats on the neck.

"Oh, good girl, good girl," she praised. "Doesn't that cold water feel good?"

As Heather continued to applaud her mare's action, Frosty lowered her head and took a big gulp of water. She then raised her head, looked around and once again, lowered her head. Taking a much longer drink this time, Frosty seemed to have an almost insatiable thirst. Finally, she raised her head, but only slightly. Then, down it went, a third time. This time, however, she stopped when her nose reached the water. Hearing a strange noise, Heather looked down to see Frosty blowing bubbles through her nose!

"What on earth are you doing?" laughed Heather. "I've never seen a horse, hey! Wait a minute, cut that out! What are you doing? Stop that!"

Everybody turned toward Heather and Frosty to see what was going on. The whole group burst out laughing, for the sight they saw was hysterical. Frosty was playing in the water and having a blast. Raising a front leg as far above the water as she possibly could, she then sent it crashing into the water with all her might, creating a huge splash. First she did it with one front leg, over and over again. Then, when that leg needed a rest, she continued the motion with her other front leg. The water was flying everywhere, but mostly onto Heather.

"Ugh! Cut it out, cut it out!" squealed Heather.

Finally, with both her and her rider drenched with cold water, Frosty decided she'd had enough. Without guidance from her rider, the mare raised her head and walked out of the water as if nothing had happened.

"That was great Heather," shouted Laura from the other side of the stream. "Will you do it again, please? We want to see it again!"

"Very funny, Laura," hollered Heather in return. "But I think I've had enough. My clothes are all wet, my saddle is probably ruined, and I have water dripping down into my face from my soaking wet hair. How about you and Rusty going for a dip?"

"Nah, I think I'll pass," smiled Laura.

With that, the group slowly turned their attention towards the beckoning trail. Heather found Sarah and Holly both grinning from ear to ear, obviously pleased with the show they'd just seen. Heather just rolled her eyes, sighed and walked right past them.

"That was great," said Sarah, as her horse trotted up to Frosty. "I used to have a mare that did the same thing. Drove me nuts but it was a good way to cool off in the summer."

The girls continued to talk as the last stretch of trail opened up before them. The warm summer air dried Heather's clothes and the incident was soon forgotten. Finally, as Heather's stomach began to grumble, announcing the approaching dinner hour, the path opened up into a large grassy field.

"Frosty was playing in the water and having a blast."

"Did we just do a loop?" asked Heather. "Isn't this the field we started in?"

"No," answered Holly. "We're several miles from that field now. Look down there," she said, pointing off in the distance. "See that pond? There wasn't a pond at the last field."

"Oh, yeah, you're right," replied Heather.

The girls rode their horses into the field where several groups of horses and riders were already gathered. There were several volunteers roaming around and these people showed the girls where to tie their horses, where their equipment had been placed and where they could pick up their dinner.

By the time Laura and Jennifer arrived at the camp, Heather and her friends had already fed their horses and were waiting in line for their dinners. Joining them as they finished up their meals, Laura and Jennifer wanted to know all about Frosty's new found love of water. They teased Heather but also congratulated her for building up Frosty's confidence.

"You know, Heather, Frosty is a completely different horse from the one you bought at the auction," noted Laura. "She's not the shy, skittish animal she once was. She trusts you and it shows."

"Yeah, I'll second that," said Jennifer. "Anybody who can take a horse that Jim Spencer once had and make it a usable animal deserves a medal!"

"Who is Jim Spencer?" asked Sarah.

Heather told Sarah and Holly the story of Mr. Spencer; how he had once gotten his hands on both of her horses, how cruel he was to his animals and how every horse that was kept in his barn wound up afraid of people. As the story concluded, the girls were interrupted by Mr. Finnery, the president of the riding club,

"Welcome to camp, everybody! I hope you all enjoyed a wonderful afternoon of riding. I just have a few matters of business to discuss and then I'll let you all continue enjoying the party. First, the second section of the ride is on a much older trail and is slightly overgrown in a few places. It is also a little more complicated than the first section, with a lot of side trails merging in and out with the main trail. Finally, instead of bright yellow ties, this section is marked with white paint on trees. These marks may be a little harder to see so you'll have to pay close attention. Having said that, this section offers some of the most spectacular views you'll ever see. The weather forecast for tomorrow is hazy, hot and humid with afternoon thunderstorms. So, please, be careful."

The rest of the evening was spent lavishing attention on the horses, strolling along the banks of the pond and playing card games. Exhausted from their busy day, everyone climbed into their sleeping bags early and by 9 PM, the camp was quiet.

The soft nicker of Frosty woke Heather early in the morning. The young girl lay with her head hidden in her sleeping bag for several minutes and then slowly emerged. Wiping the sleep from her eyes, Heather looked around to see a thick mist of fog surrounding her. Slowly rising from her sleeping bag, Heather could barely make out the body of Frosty, just twenty feet away from her. The damp, cool air gave Heather goosebumps and sent a chill down her spine. Quickly grabbing Frosty's grain and hay from a pile of supplies that had been gathered the night before, Heather fed her mare and crawled back into her sleeping bag. The sound of rustling hay aroused the attention of other horses and with that, the camp came to life.

After breakfast, Heather tacked up her mare and was ready to get started. She couldn't wait to get going and was frustrated because Laura and Jennifer were still eating their breakfast.

"I'm going to ride down around the pond for a little bit," said Heather as she rode Frosty passed Laura and Jennifer, who were involved in a friendly argument about a horse.

"Sure, have fun," replied Laura, who really wasn't paying attention to Heather.

Heather rode her mare towards the pond, which was difficult to find, given the heavy fog. The trail that the group was to take today started near the pond but with the thick mist hiding everything, Heather had a hard time finding it. Still, with a little work, she was able to find the trail and followed it down to the pond. Walking along the edge, Heather was enjoying the natural beauty of the area, with a stillness that was both scary and beautiful at the same time. She could hear people and horses off in the distance, but because of the fog, she couldn't see them. She felt alone and yet safe.

Suddenly, Frosty lifted her head high into the air. She froze, stared and then blew out through her nose.

"What's there, girl?"

Frosty blew again.

Heather squinted, trying to see through the fog. Suddenly she saw the object of Frosty's attention. A large deer, with a grace that Heather had never seen before, was walking along the opposite side of the pond. Seeing the horse and rider, the deer paused, then slowly lifted a front leg and held it slightly above the ground. Frosty blew out through her nose again and the noise, frightening the deer, made it jump in fear. In a moment it was off, running along the edge of the pond.

"Come on girl, let's race!" cried Heather as she urged her mare to run.

The deer continued at an easy pace towards the end of the pond where it must have seen the opening to the woods created by the trail. This was the same trail Frosty was running along. It was easier for the girl and her horse to cover ground quickly as the deer had to jump over several fallen logs and cover much more uneven terrain. As the deer reached the end of the pond, it picked up the trail, just several feet in front of Frosty.

Although it was hard to see because of the fog, Heather was able to keep the deer in sight. Instead of leaving the trail, it continued along the path, jumping from side to side and waving its big, white tail in front of Frosty as a distraction. Heather squealed in delight as she'd never dreamt of running alongside a deer. The trail was rutted with tree roots in several places and Frosty slipped and tripped a few times but was unwilling to slow down. She had decided this was a new game, and was eager to overtake the deer and lead the pack. The trail weaved around large trees and up and down small hills. At one point, the trail crossed a stream and the deer simply and gracefully cleared it in a single jump. In contrast, Frosty splashed through the water, splattering Heather with the cool liquid.

As the chase continued, Heather was amazed that the deer didn't veer off the trail into more secluded areas. Perhaps this lovely animal was enjoying the game just as much as she and Frosty. Whatever the reason, the game continued until the deer entered what appeared to be the same field where they had started the chase. It was hard for Heather to tell for sure as the fog prevented her from seeing more than twenty feet ahead of her.

Without any urging, Frosty continued to follow the deer at a fast pace through the field. Galloping to the far end, where the trees once again met the field, the deer jumped through a thicket of bushes and instantly disappeared. Frosty would have crashed through the bushes had it not been for Heather, who pulled tight on the reins. The mare raised her head high and opened her mouth, trying to evade the tight pressure of the bit, and was forced to stop.

"I think that's enough, Frosty. I can't see the deer any more and there's no trail here. I think we lost her."

Heather turned her mare back in the direction they had come. Frosty was huffing and puffing from the early morning workout and was now happy to be walking. As they took several strides, Heather slowly looked around her. The fog was thick and unrelenting. There was no trail to follow, no human voices or horse whinnies in the distance. Heather suddenly couldn't tell from which direction they had come. Then she realized...they were lost!

CHAPTER TEN

LOST!

Silence. Total and complete silence. There were no birds singing, no crickets chirping, nothing. The only sound was the creaking of the leather saddle as Heather shifted her weight slightly, turning this way and that, trying to see through the dense fog. What she saw frightened her. A white veil of thick mist covered the ground and rose up all around her. It seemed even thicker than the fog down along the pond where their foolish game had started. A chill shot down Heather's spine. She was scared and didn't know what to do.

Frosty, on the other hand, was quite content. As Heather looked around, trying to discern any familiar landmark, Frosty had pulled her head forward in an attempt to loosen Heather's grasp on the reins. Not paying attention to her horse, the reins slipped through her hands and she let them flop on Frosty's neck. Happy to have the tight reins loosened, Frosty immediately dropped her head and began eating the lush grass that surrounded her.

As Frosty continued to eat, Heather continued to look around her. She was afraid of going anywhere, as her sense of direction was totally gone. She thought they were facing the direction they had come from, but she wasn't sure. What if she was wrong? She might wind up traveling in the wrong direction and getting herself even further into trouble.

"Hello?" she suddenly yelled at the top of her lungs. "Hello! Is anybody there?"

The unexpected noise startled Frosty, whose head shot up. A flock of birds (or was it something else?), also frightened by the noise, flew up from the ground, nearby but unseen. This noise, in turn, surprised Frosty who jumped sideways. With reins flopping, Frosty was free to turn and run, which she started to do. Heather, caught off guard, lost her balance and had to grab a chunk of Frosty's mane in order to keep from falling. Instantly gathering up the reins, she managed to bring Frosty to a halt after only a few frantic steps.

"Easy girl, easy," said Heather as she stroked Frosty's neck. "It's okay. There's nothing there." Looking up as she said that, Heather didn't believe her own words. There was something there. "We better get going."

With that, Heather gently tapped Frosty's sides with her legs and the mare obediently began to walk forward. Unfortunately, when Frosty had jumped, she had also turned to the side, so the pair were now headed further into the depths of the Vermont woods, not back towards camp...

****

"Heather, come on, let's go!" hollered Laura as she and Rusty slowly made their way to the pond. The fog was still thick and soupy and it was impossible to see more than twenty feet in any one direction. Laura heard a horse approach and turned, expecting to see Heather.

160

"I thought she said she was going with Sarah and Holly," came the voice.

"Is that you, Jennifer?" asked Laura, unable to see anybody but recognizing the voice.

"Yeah, it's me," replied Jennifer. "Didn't Heather say she was going to ride with Sarah and Holly today? I thought that's what she said at dinner last night."

"I must have missed that. Have they started out on the trail already? Do you know?"

"I saw Holly about half an hour ago. She was all tacked up and ready to leave, so I guess they must have left."

"Man," grumbled Laura, "Heather is going to be in so much trouble tonight when I see her. I don't mind her riding with her new friends, but she needs to tell me when she's leaving. Come on, we better get started too. I don't hear any other riders; we must be the last ones to hit the trail. Let's go."

With that, Laura and Jennifer set out for a fun day of trail riding. They would spend the day enjoying their horses, the incredible scenery and their renewed friendship. Not once during that time would they worry about Heather.

****

Heather slowly made her way to the edge of the field, still unable to see anything through the dense fog. She wanted to have Frosty run as fast as the mare could, just like she had while chasing the deer. Somehow, perhaps, Frosty would run in the right direction and get them out of this mess. But Heather knew that running was a bad idea. The grass was tall and wet from the heavy mist and the weight of the dampness forced the grass to flop over in big clumps. These clumps made the ground feel uneven to Frosty's hooves and the mare had to lower her head and pay close attention to avoid tripping. These big clusters of flopping grass also made it possible to conceal groundhog holes or other hazards that might normally be seen. So cautious, slow progress was a necessity.

The field seemed to go on forever and Heather was certain that they hadn't traveled so far, even at a full gallop. Should she turn around? Could she even be sure that they were going in a straight line? What if they were walking in a slightly crooked line? Then they'd really be messed up. What should she do?

Heather asked Frosty to stop and the mare obediently came to a halt. As the mare snatched a morning snack, her rider looked around her, first to the left, then to the right. The fog gave no signs of letting up and Heather was becoming more confused by the minute. Which way should they go?

After what seemed like an eternity, Heather decided to continue on their present path. This field couldn't go on forever. Once they found the woods, they'd surely find the trail that would lead them home.

Finally, after several more anxious minutes, Frosty stumbled into a low-lying bush. She tried to walk right over it but the bush was too wide and thick. Frosty hesitated for a moment, and than decided to go around it. As she did so, Heather asked her to stop. Looking ahead of her, the frightened girl saw several trees. They had reached the woods. There was no trail entrance here but perhaps it was just several feet away. Should they turn to the left or right? In which direction might the trail be? Without thinking, Heather urged her mare to head to the left and so they continued, looking for the trail entrance.

Once again, the pair proceeded slowly around the field, although this time they traveled along the edge, next to the woods. Heather kept her eye on the trees, looking for any possible sign of a trail. The fog, unrelenting in its determination to cast a thick veil of white soup throughout the field, made the search almost impossible. Heather wanted to call out, over and over, to see if anybody was around. But somehow, with the silence so profound, she was too frightened. It felt as though somebody was there, watching her, somebody whom she didn't want to find her. She clutched a tuft of her horse's mane tightly, ready to hold on tight should the animal jump again. There was no way that she would be separated from Frosty. Not here, not now.

Horse and rider continued to walk around the field but there was no sign of a trail entrance. Perhaps they had already walked by it but had failed to notice it, with all the fog hiding any hints of a path. Or maybe they had not come to it yet. But it seemed as though they should have found the trail by now, and Heather was sure that she'd already seen the birch tree in front of them, with its unique white bark and large, fallen branch. They were now going in circles.

"What am I going to do?" she whispered to herself. Then suddenly, it hit her. How silly, how wonderful! Why hadn't she thought of it before? Her cell phone!

With a smile emerging on her face, Heather reached into the front saddlebag and pulled out her cell phone. Eagerly she snapped it open and turned it on. The dial tone that buzzed was one of the most wonderful sounds she had ever heard. She dialed Laura's cell phone number.

"Beep, beep, beep, beep, beep..."

The sound of a cell phone that is unable to reach a tower, a phone without reception.

"Message 294," came the monotone voice. "No service available at this time."

"Oh, no," groaned Heather. "How can that be? I thought we'd have service up here all the time."

The smile quickly turned to a frown, but now determination was taking over.

"We're just going to have to go somewhere else then, Frosty. We'll ride until we can get service on this stupid cell phone."

Again, the dilemma of which direction to go surfaced. Heather knew that the sun rose in the east and set in the west and that could help her get back. But with the fog so thick, she couldn't see the sun. Was it even out? Or was it hiding behind some early morning clouds? There was no way to know.

"Well, we've got to go someplace girl," said Heather to her horse. "And I don't know about you, but I'm tired of this field. Let's get out of here."

With that, Heather guided her horse into the woods, crashing through some underbrush next to the birch tree.

Once in the woods, progress was slow as the pair weaved in, out and around the trees that stood in their way. As they continued, the trees grew larger, taller, and thicker while the underbrush slowly disappeared. The trees here were big, with branches and needles that seemed to spread out forever. With so many outstretched limbs, the sun was unable to break through to give life to the small bushes below and so, only fallen branches and rocks blocked the way.

Heather's stomach began to grumble. It was time for her mid-morning snack. She pulled Frosty to a halt and reached into her saddlebag. Pulling out a granola bar, she ripped the wrapping off and devoured the entire contents in three big mouthfuls. Next she took a huge mouthful of water from her bottle, the one that she had filled before leaving on her deer chase. Placing the wrapper back into the saddlebag, Heather looked into the bag and was dismayed to see only two remaining granola bars. She would have to spread her next meal out much longer if she was to get home before running out of food.

Frosty deserved a rest too, but her rider was too frightened to get off. The mare would have to settle for loose reins and a pat on the neck. As Heather sat on top of her horse, looking around, she realized that the fog was burning off. Visibility was getting much better!

While Heather looked about, the fog seemed to dissipate before her eyes. Within minutes, Heather could see far off into the distance. Unfortunately, all she saw were more trees. No path, no people, no houses, nothing. Dismayed but not willing to give up, Heather pulled out her cell phone and tried to call Laura again.

"Beep, beep, beep, beep, beep..."

"Still no service," grumbled the girl. "Come on Frosty, let's keep going."

As the fog lifted and more of her surroundings became visible, Heather felt her fear subside somewhat. Seeing that there was nothing following her, nothing hiding behind a tree or bush, nothing lurking in the branches above her, gave her a sense of safety. Although the thick covering of leaves overhead hid the blue sky, there were specks of sunlight that managed to break through. Brightening up the forest with sunshine, however meager, brought several birds out of their hiding places. As they jumped from branch to branch, they began chirping. At the same time, all sorts of bugs and insects ventured beyond their damp homes to sun themselves and enjoy the heat of the day. Birds sang, bees buzzed, deerflies landed on Frosty for a snack, grasshoppers rubbed their legs together in song and squirrels ran back and forth between trees, scurrying from one to another with amazing speed. The forest had come to life.

Now that the landscape was visible, Frosty was able to pick up her pace quite a bit. She worked her way among the fallen limbs, tree roots and rocks with great agility and speed. The young gray mare was completely relaxed and happy to be out enjoying a ride with her owner. Her head was carried proudly, neck arched and raised slightly but not as high as a Morgan who was in the show ring. She had to watch where she was going and therefore kept her eyes focused on the ground ahead of her. Heather kept her reins loose, gently guiding the mare left, and then right, as needed to avoid hitting a low-hanging branch or other obstacle.

As the pair continued on their journey, the heat and humidity that Mr. Finnery had predicted for the day began in earnest. It was hot! The perspiration dripped down Heather's forehead, the back of her neck was wet and she was thirsty. Frosty was hot too. The mare's neck was drenched in sweat, even though they were traveling at a slow walk. The sweat attracted all sorts of blood-sucking insects who were anxious for a meal. They swarmed around Frosty, looking for the perfect spot to land. Heather was forced to continually shoo them away. Unfortunately, as soon as the pests were chased away, they would turn around and attack again. As more and more of them gathered for a feast, they found Heather's ankles which were unprotected due to her short socks. Zooming around her legs, they next found her back and kept trying to grab a snack through her t-shirt. Heather was miserable and Frosty was quickly following suit.

"I need to find you some water," said Heather as she shooed yet another group of deerflies away.

As they wandered around, perhaps going in circles, Heather looked for a stream but none was in sight. She knew Frosty had to be thirsty.

"Whoa, girl. I need to stop for a minute."

Frosty stopped and Heather, feeling a little more secure now that she could see her surroundings, dismounted. Uncomfortable from the heat, Heather took off her riding helmet and wiped the sweat away with the damp fabric of her t-shirt. As flies buzzed around, she was once again forced to chase them away. Then she carefully grabbed a small amount of skin from Frosty's neck and pulled it away from the mare's body. Immediately, Heather released the section of hide. The skin slowly fell back into place against the mare's side. This was a simple test that Chauncy had taught Heather when she first began riding his horses. The skin on a normal, well-hydrated horse jumps back into place instantly. Only on a thirsty, dehydrated horse does it go back into place slowly.

It wouldn't be long before Frosty began to show other signs of dehydration.

"I need to find you some water now."

Looking around, Heather hoped to see a stream that she had somehow missed during her first inspection of this area. Nothing.

"Well, I can't wait. You'll have to have some of my water," said Heather as she reached into her saddlebag and pulled out her water bottle. The riding helmet would have been a perfect container for water, but unfortunately, it had several long, open slots. These slots greatly improved ventilation but made the helmet a poor choice to hold water. Realizing this, Heather put it down on the ground so she could more easily use her hands.

"Here you go, Frosty."

Heather squirted a small amount of water onto her hand. Frosty immediately noticed the water, muzzled it gently and spilling more than she drank, guzzled down all that she could. Heather squirted more water into her hand and Frosty kept her mouth against her owner's hand, taking in the water as soon as it hit the hand. Again and again Heather fed her mare water until her bottle was almost empty.

"That's all I can spare, Frosty. Come on, we better get going."

As Heather mounted, she heard the roar of thunder off in the distance. The huge trees continued to block out the sky so Heather couldn't tell if storm clouds were moving in but as another boom of thunder was heard, she knew a storm was approaching.

"We better find some cover," she said to her mare.

Heather spotted an enormous pine tree, with a huge trunk and many low-lying branches. She knew that being next to a tree during a thunder storm was a bad idea, but what should you do when you're stuck in a forest full of trees? She didn't know the answer, but as another blast of thunder was heard, this time much closer, Heather didn't waste any time. She dismounted and led Frosty to the tree.

As the two friends stood underneath the tree, the rain began. At first it was just a slow spattering. One drop here, one drop there, one on Heather's head and one on her saddle. The air grew still and the light disappeared as the forest grew dark. Suddenly the intensity of the rain picked up and within seconds, the spattering had turned into a torrential downpour. Even with the thick covering of pine needles above, the rain poured through. As the rain mixed with Heather's sweat and slid down her face, the mixture made its way into the thirsty girl's mouth. Although salty to the tasty, the liquid brought welcome relief. Thinking quickly, Heather grabbed her almost empty water bottle from the saddlebag, screwed off the cap and held it high, hoping to capture some fresh water.

Frosty kept her head low and stood quietly next to Heather. The woods flashed bright for an instant, followed by an ear-piercing crash. Frosty jumped, frightened by this loud monster that was coming towards them. Heather too, was frightened. She had never been out in the woods during a thunderstorm, and the intensity of this one would have frightened her even within the safety of her home.

Heather and Frosty cowered under the tree together. The storm was upon them. Another lightening flash appeared, followed once again by the earsplitting noise of thunder. At the same time, the sound of a tree splintering apart and crashing to the ground was heard in the distance. Heather dropped her water bottle and drew closer to her horse, grabbing the mare's mane for comfort. Frosty, seeming to sense the terror her owner was experiencing, stood perfectly still and gently muzzled Heather's stomach. The frightened girl jumped as another bright flash appeared and thunder boomed through the woods.

Just as fast as the storm had approached, it continued on its path and hurriedly passed through the area. A few more close flashes of lightening and then the noise of the thunder diminished as the storm drifted away. The rain stopped and within minutes, the woods brightened as the sun above fought away the storm clouds.

Heather looked around her. Everything was soaking wet, including her, her horse and her saddle. The water on her face and clothes felt refreshing as she walked Frosty out from underneath the tree and climbed back into the saddle. As she clucked to her mare, Heather remembered her water bottle. Heather immediately stopped her mare, jumped down, ran to the tree and found her water bottle among the damp needles on the ground. The bottle was now half full of water. The thirsty girl took a small sip and then mounted her horse.

While Frosty walked along, Heather pulled out her cell phone. She was about to dial Laura's number when she noticed that the screen was blank. She hit the power button and the screen

"The storm was upon them."

flashed on for just a moment. Heather stared in disbelief as she saw a low battery message appear for a split second before the screen went blank again. Leaving her phone on since yesterday had drained the battery and she had lost power. Now her phone was useless.

As the lost travelers continued, the heat and humidity that had bothered them so much before the storm reappeared. Heather's damp clothes now stuck to her body and the annoying biting insects zeroed in on the pair. Once again, the misery of being eaten by bloodthirsty pests began.

Heather wiped the sweat from her forehead and as she did so she suddenly realized that her riding helmet was gone. Where was it? Then she remembered - she had put it down when she stopped to water Frosty. But that was before the storm and they had traveled quite a bit since then. There was no way she could find the helmet now. It was gone.

Heather continued to lead her horse in what she thought was the same direction, although they were actually traveling in a pattern that more closely resembled a squiggly line. The trees were slowly thinning out and becoming younger and thus, smaller. Maybe they were getting close to a field, thought Heather. Maybe the base camp field!

Frosty made her way to the top of what appeared to be a little hill. Before them was a small valley, with steep walls to each side.

"That looks promising," said Heather. "Let's go there."

The gray mare obediently made her way down the hill into the valley. As they reached the bottom, Frosty noticed that the grass at the edge of this valley was thick and juicy. Eager for some food, she pulled her head down and began to eat. Heather, seeing how hungry her mare was, dismounted and let Frosty graze for a while.

While Frosty ate, Heather grabbed another granola bar from her saddlebag and consumed it quickly. It had to be well past lunchtime and she was hungry too! Once the appetites of both human and equine had been satisfied, Heather mounted and asked Frosty to move on. The mare took several steps and then stopped.

"What's wrong Frosty? Come on, let's go."

Frosty took a few more steps and then stopped again. Heather looked down to see that the mare's feet had sunk into a little mud.

"Oh, come on, now. That's ridiculous!" scolded Heather. "You're not going to let a little mud scare you, are you? Come on, get going!"

Heather kicked her mare gently but the horse still refused to go. Heather kicked again. Still Frosty refused. The mare was agitated and began to paw with her left front leg.

"Frosty," commanded Heather, in a stern voice, "move!"

Heather kicked her mare again, this time harder than before.

The mare reluctantly went forward and her legs sank into more and more mud as they continued. Heather looked in front of them and thought she saw a stream in the distance.

"Water!" she shouted. "Come on Frosty, let's get going!"

Frosty took several more steps and then suddenly her body dropped down. They were in a swamp! The mud rushed around the mare's legs, covering everything below her knees. Heather, realizing what was happening, asked her mare to turn around before it was too late. Frosty tried to move but she couldn't. In desperation, Heather pulled at the reins with all her might, trying to force Frosty's head, and thus her body, to turn. As she did so, Heather unknowingly turned her own body in anticipation of Frosty's turn. But Frosty, unable to turn, instead managed to jump forward in an awkward attempt to escape the mud. The combination of the turn on her part and the jump on her mare's part made Heather lose her balance. She fell forward and in an instant she was on the ground, right in front of Frosty. The mare, already in motion, couldn't stop her movement and so, jumped over Heather. Unfortunately, only Frosty's front legs managed to pass over Heather. The back legs, unable to move very far, were behind the girl. Heather was now trapped underneath her mare!

Stunned by what had happened in a moment's time, Heather lay motionless. Her horse was now up to her belly in mud and Heather was trapped beneath that belly. The mud below Heather cushioned her and as she sank down a bit, she was able to breath without any trouble. But she couldn't move. Frosty, meanwhile, looked about her, not knowing what to do, not understanding why Heather was lying below her.

Heather quickly understood her dilemma and was terrified. She couldn't move her head, nor her arms or legs that were held in place beneath her horse. The frightened girl was afraid that the mud would slowly drag her down below the surface.

"Help me, help me!" yelled the girl at the top of her lungs.

The loud, panicked scream scared the horse and forced the mare into action. Frosty let out a big groan from the depths of her body and then focused all her attention on moving. She gathered all her strength into her hind legs and forced them up. Heather, seeing that her mare was about to jump again, closed her eyes in fear. Another groan, some movement, a splashing sound and then the weight from Heather's chest was gone. The frightened girl opened her eyes to see Frosty about ten feet ahead of her. The mare was standing next to a small sapling, on a mound of dirt that rose above the swamp. Heather could feel herself shaking as she slowly sat up, astonished that she was still alive.

As Heather stumbled out of the mud, she rushed over to her mare who was trembling with fear.

"I'm so sorry," cried Heather. "I'm so sorry. I should have listened to you. You knew this wasn't a safe place, that's why you wouldn't go. I'm so sorry," whimpered the girl as she stroked the horse's neck.

Heather checked every part of her horse, from her legs to her head, making sure there were no signs of injury. Only after she was sure that Frosty was all right, did she turn her attention to herself. Her back and sides were covered with mud but her front was relatively clean. A spattering of brown goo here and there, but otherwise, nothing. Then Heather noticed the mark on her chest. In amazement she stared at the muddy hoofprint that adorned her t-shirt. She hadn't felt Frosty step on her and couldn't understand why it didn't hurt. Maybe she was too stunned to feel the pain or maybe the mud had cushioned the impact; Heather didn't know.

Whatever the reason, Heather was just glad it didn't hurt.

Turning her attention back to Frosty, Heather once again checked for injuries. Seeing none, she stroked the mare's neck and promised to never doubt the faithful horse again.

"Now, how do we get out of here?"

Heather looked around and for the first time noticed that this area was covered, not with the sweet, juicy grass like that Frosty had been eating earlier, but with swamp grass. It grew in clumps, with a very narrow, rounded shape that allowed the blades to stand upright and not flop over. The clumps were everywhere; how could she not have noticed them? Dismayed, Heather searched for a way out. A few feet in front of her, off to the side, there appeared to be some sweet grass and that's where the girl headed. She let Frosty stay next to the small sapling until a way out was found.

Trudging through knee-high mud, Heather made her way to the grassy mound. Seeing that it was safe, she returned to Frosty and guided the mare to the drier spot. Once there, Heather saw that they couldn't go back, the muck was too deep. They couldn't go up the sides of the valley, as it was much too steep and rocky. They would have to follow the edge of the swamp to the other side.

Their progress out of the swamp was painfully slow. Heather could easily see what she thought was the end of the swamp, where small trees were growing and the grass looked more inviting. But not wanting to make the same mistake twice, Heather traveled cautiously. She checked the placement of each foot twice before putting any weight on the ground and only asked her mare to move when she was sure it was safe.

Frosty too, was reluctant to move without testing the earth below her hooves and was happy to travel at a slow pace.

Finally the friends reached the end of the swamp. The ground rose slightly and hardened into solid footing. Heather eagerly picked up her pace, relieved to be away from the mud. Walking over a small hill, she was thrilled to find a stream, with clear fast moving water rushing over the small rocks in its path.

"Frosty! Water!" she squealed as she raced to the edge of the stream.

Frosty was just as excited to see the water as her owner. Trotting behind the girl, the mare eagerly dropped her head into the water and felt the cool, refreshing liquid drench her lips.

"Not too fast, girl, not too fast. I don't want you to get sick."

The mare continued to drink at a frantic pace and Heather was afraid that she would make herself sick. Reluctantly, she forced the mare's head up, then waited a minute before allowing Frosty to drink again. Over and over Heather repeated this action until her horse had had enough to drink.

Once their thirst had been quenched, Heather made the decision to stop for a long rest. They had been traveling all day and, judging by her stomach grumbles, it was approaching dinnertime. Heather removed the bit and reins from Frosty's bridle with a few simple snaps, and converted Frosty's bridle into a halter. Then she reattached one of the reins to a ring on Frosty's halter. Heather looped the rein around Frosty's neck, hoping the feeling of the rein would be enough to keep the mare from running off.

Just like the far edge of the swamp, the grass here was abundant and Frosty quickly got to work. Meanwhile, Heather took off her socks and sneakers and washed them in the stream. Then she sat at the edge of the water, toes wiggling in the stream, arms outstretched behind her, propping her body up. Her head was tilted up, eyes closed, taking in the warm rays of the sun. Suddenly it hit her...

"The sun! The sun! Frosty, I can see the sun!"

Frosty raised her head, stared at Heather for a moment and then decided the grass was far more important than anything the girl was saying.

"The sun is starting to set, and it sets in the west. That means that south is that way," noted Heather as she pointed in the direction the stream was flowing, "which is that way we want to go, I think. Chauncy always said that if you get lost, find a stream and follow it. A stream will always go somewhere, eventually."

Heather got up, walked over to Frosty and pulled the last granola bar from the saddlebag. She returned to her spot on the grass and ate her dinner as slowly as possible. She wanted every bite to last. Now she was thirsty. Returning to the saddlebag, Heather pulled out her water bottle and took several big gulps. She drank almost all the water but there was no need to ration it; she had a stream with clear running water at her disposal. Heather screwed open the cap, walked over to the water and bent down to fill the bottle. But just as she was about to dip the bottle into the stream she stopped. How did she know the water was safe? Just because it looked clean didn't mean it was. It could be filled with all sorts of bacteria. Instead of just being lost, thought Heather, if she drank that water she might get really sick.

Heather decided not to drink from the stream. She would follow it out of the woods and hopefully make it to civilization before she needed another drink.

Feeling relaxed and ready to continue the journey home, Heather rose, grabbed her damp socks and sneakers and was about to mount her horse when she realized that it was growing dark. Heather was afraid to stay in the woods alone at night but it appeared that she would have no choice. Looking into the dark woods reminded her of the early morning fog. She couldn't see what was hiding beyond the first few trees and it terrified her. However, seeing that this spot was in the open made her feel more secure, although whether it truly was safer to sleep out in the open she didn't know. But she decided to camp here, next to the stream. Hopefully the night would pass quickly...

****

"Heather, you are going to be in so much trouble," exclaimed Laura as she and Rusty approached a gray mare and girl from behind. They had traveled all day without running into Heather, Holly or Sarah, and now that they were at camp, Laura's first priority was to find Heather and give her heck. "You can't imagine what I'm going to say to you, let alone what your mother will say when she finds out!"

"Huh?" asked a pony-tailed girl as she turned around to see Laura.

"Oh, sorry. I thought you were somebody else," said Laura as she realized this girl wasn't Heather.

Laura continued to ride Rusty around the camp, looking for Heather. She was starting to get worried. Finally she found Holly and Sarah, already consuming their dinners.

"Hey guys!" exclaimed Laura. "I'm so glad I found you. Where's Heather?"

"We don't know," answered Sarah. "We haven't seen her all day. Didn't she ride with you?"

"No, we thought she was with you two," replied Laura.

Sarah and Holly just shook their heads.

"Oh my gosh!" cried out Laura as she turned her horse and ran off.

****

As Heather drifted off to an uneasy sleep, a search party was being organized twenty miles away. Police, volunteers and dogs were called in to look for the lost girl, and at the break of dawn, an airplane would join in the hunt.

When morning came, Heather woke up covered with bite marks. Sleeping next to a stream, with a swamp not far away, had invited all the neighborhood mosquitoes to an evening snack. They had come in droves and kept waking Heather up with their low buzzing sounds and annoying bites. She had tried to cover herself with grass and old leaves but still the insects found their prey. Now her whole body itched.

Walking over to the stream, Heather cupped her hands in the water and brought the cool liquid over her face, being careful not to drink any. Next she washed her arms and ankles as best she could. Frosty, meanwhile had been tied to a tree at the edge of the woods and was trying to nibble at the grass just out of reach. She had eaten

180

everything around the tree during the night and was now eager to eat more. Heather knew that they couldn't set out before Frosty had breakfast, as her energy was required for the long day ahead.

Heather allowed Frosty to eat for quite a while before getting started. When it was time to leave, Heather had difficulty getting her mare ready. Frosty was reluctant to have the bit put back as it interfered with her eating, and fought Heather's attempts to insert it into her mouth. Finally, after a few tries, Heather was able to get it in. With the saddle on and the halter converted back into a bridle, they were ready to get started.

The stream disappeared into the woods a few hundred feet beyond their camp and it was there that they began the day's journey.

Following the stream through the woods, up and down gullies, around trees and through thickets, made for very slow going. It was hard for Frosty to maneuver through some of the areas, particularly those close to the stream that had a lot of mud. Frosty was now hesitant to go anywhere near mud and Heather had no intention of forcing her. As the sun above approached its peak, Heather's stomach announced the lunch hour. Actually, her stomach had been grumbling all morning but there was nothing the girl could do.

Slowly, the stream got smaller and smaller until it completely disappeared. Disappointed but refusing to give up, Heather continued to ride her mare in the direction that she guessed might lead to civilization. Before long, the terrain became rather rocky and steep. There were large and small rocks everywhere as well as plenty of tiny little pebbles scattered throughout. This difficult landscape made progress quite difficult. Heather, getting frustrated at their slow pace, was just about to turn around when she spotted a large tree at the top of a small knoll. The branches of the tree were set in such a way as to make it perfect for climbing. Heather thought that if she climbed up the tree, she might be able to spot some landmark, such as a road or house.

"Let's stop here, Frosty," suggested Heather.

Seeing that it was once again time for a snack, Frosty eagerly stopped and waited for Heather to convert the mare's bridle into a halter. Once the bit was removed, Frosty began to search the hill for grass and was disappointed at the lack of lush green growth.

While Frosty searched for food, Heather decided to climb the tree. Hopping up onto a nearby rock, Heather easily climbed onto the first branch of the tree. Within minutes she was high up, peering down at her surroundings. Looking at her horse, she could see that Frosty had found something that caught her attention. The mare was standing next to one of the big rocks, head down, nuzzling something that seemed to be moving.

"Hey Frosty, what's there? What did you find?" Looking up, she continued, "Wow, Frosty, you should see the view from up here. Hey!" she exclaimed suddenly, "Frosty, I think I see a road, and, and, and a house! Frosty, can you believe it? I think we've found a way out of..."

Just then Frosty let out an ear-piercing scream...

CHAPTER ELEVEN

SOLVING THE MYSTERY

Heather had never heard a horse scream before. The noise was a combination of a loud whinny and high-pitched squeal. There was no doubt in Heather's mind that Frosty was in extreme pain. It was also obvious to the girl that the mare was confused and terrified.

Heather looked down to see something long, thin and round slither under a rock. In the same instant, her mare pulled herself back from the rock, threw her head high into the air, turned and then ran off in a frantic effort to get away from whatever it was that had scared her. The reins, still attached to the halter, flew behind the mare as she disappeared into the distance.

"Frosty, no! Wait! Don't leave me!" screamed Heather as she scrambled down the tree as fast as she could. Shaking from the excitement of the moment, Heather's foot slipped as it reached for the lowest branch on the tree and the girl lost her balance. Losing her hold, Heather's whole body came tumbling down and hit the ground hard. Landing first on her side, then her shoulder, Heather's head then met the ground. Everything went black as Heather dropped into unconsciousness.

Waking up several minutes later (or was it hours?), Heather lay still for a while. Her head hurt, her ears were ringing, and she was afraid she might have broken a bone or two. Lying on the hard ground, Heather first wiggled her fingers. No pain. Next she moved her toes. Again, no pain. Slowly testing the rest of her body, Heather was relieved to find nothing broken, nothing in excruciating pain. She decided to sit up. Raising herself slowly, Heather was overcome with dizziness and nausea. The world around her seemed to be spinning and her ears were ringing louder and louder.

Still sitting, Heather pushed herself backwards just a bit so that she could use the large rock behind her as a brace. Leaning against the hard surface, she closed her eyes and waited. Gradually, the ringing in her ears lessened. Not moving a muscle, Heather cautiously opened her eyes. Looking around her, she was relieved to find that the dizziness and nausea had subsided too. All that remained was a small headache. Resting for a few more minutes, Heather slowly got to her feet. Still leaning against the rock, she called out to her horse, "Frosty, Frosty, where are you?"

Silence.

"Frosty? Can you hear me?"

A crow screeched in the distance.

Heather had seen the direction her mare had headed before falling from the tree and so she decided to follow, hoping to find the animal. Walking slowly so as not to make her head hurt more, Heather began her trek, searching for Frosty. The ground in this area was rather barren and there were several hoof prints visible. Heather followed the trail; it appeared that Frosty was headed back towards the stream. As the girl walked along, she called out for her horse but there was no answer.

As Heather walked around a huge rock, she heard a soft nicker. Turning the corner, she was relieved to see her horse, caught in a thicket of thorn bushes. The reins, which Heather had kept snapped to each other, had caught on a fallen branch and ensnared the horse. The reins were twisted around the branch and also entwined around one of the mare's front legs. Frosty, with her head forced down, trembled in fear.

"Easy girl, easy. I'm here," softly said Heather, trying to calm her horse. "Let's get you out of here and then you'll be fine."

It was hard to untangle the reins as the branch that held them was in the midst of the thorn bushes. Every attempt to release the reins was met with a nasty prick from a thorn.

"Ouch, that hurt," grumbled the girl to herself. She drew her hand back, shook it a few times and then put her ring finger into her mouth so she could suck the small amount of blood away. "Let's try that again."

Cautiously she tried again, slowly moving her hand toward the reins. Frosty didn't move a muscle. Perhaps she understood that she needed to stay perfectly still to be released.

"Got it!" exclaimed Heather as she withdrew her hand from the mess of bushes, while holding the reins. Leaning down, she asked Frosty to raise her front leg so she could also untangle the mare's leg from the reins.

Staring directly at Frosty's face for the first time, Heather was frightened by what she saw. The mare's nose was swollen and the rest of her face had begun to swell. Looking carefully at Frosty's nose, Heather could see two small marks.

"Those look like bite marks," mumbled Heather.

Suddenly she understood. The loud, ear-piercing scream that Frosty had let out back at the tree was caused by a snake - a snake that had bitten her!

"Oh, Frosty, we've got to get you to a vet!" cried Heather, frightened at the prospect of her beloved mare falling ill.

Frosty didn't move. There was fear and pain in her eyes and it scared Heather. Keeping her head low, Frosty just stared into space, as if she didn't know anybody was there with her.

"Come on girl, let's head towards that house I saw. We can make it, I know we can."

Reluctant to move, Heather had to pull at the reins several times to force the mare to take a step. Once moving, however, Frosty continued to slowly follow the girl without having to be prodded any more. The gray mare kept her head low and silently followed, not once looking off to either side at the sites and sounds around her. It was as if the horse was in a trance.

As they continued, Heather began to feel weak. Her headache was getting worse, the ringing in her ears was coming back, she was thirsty, and her stomach was grumbling from lack of food while at the same time, she felt as if she might vomit. She didn't know how much longer she could continue. Frosty, meanwhile had begun to breath louder. Heather turned to look at her mare and was shocked to see that the swelling had increased. Frosty's whole head was now swollen, her eyelids and even her ears were puffy and it looked as if her neck was beginning to swell. The most frightening thing, however, was that Frosty was beginning to have trouble breathing. The swelling, if it were to continue, might cut off the mare's airway and suffocate the horse. They had to get help!

Heather forced herself to turn away from her horse and continue to head in the direction of the house. As they continued, the sparse, rocky terrain gave way to small saplings and clumps of grass. Before long, the saplings were replaced by larger trees and the grass gave way to pine needles and fallen leaves. They were once again traveling through a wooded area.

"Frosty, do you hear that? Do you hear it?" asked Heather as the sound of a plane buzzed overhead. Excited at the thought of somebody flying a plane in the area, Heather had no way to know that it was a search plane and that they were searching for her. Unfortunately, tall pine trees, thick with branches, surrounded Heather and Frosty and there was no way anybody in a plane would see them. As the sound of the plane rapidly faded, Heather's excitement turned to disappointment.

"We're never going to get out of here, Frosty," whimpered the girl.

Heather, feeling as though she might collapse at any moment, forced herself to keep going. She knew they had to be close to the house, and if she gave up now, then her mare might die. She had to find that house, and get help.

The frightened girl once again turned her attention to the woods in front of her. She was dismayed to see a small hill, which looked slightly wet and slippery, in front of them. How would they ever get up that? Just as she was about to give up and look for a way around this obstacle, Heather noticed a cement tunnel at the base of it. There was water trickling through the tunnel, and looking up, Heather could now see a road at the top of the hill.

"We made it girl!" exclaimed Heather.

Feeling a sudden burst of energy, Heather quickened her pace as she eagerly headed towards the hill. Frosty grunted as she was forced to follow.

The climb up this little hill was slow. Heather had to grab at the small saplings growing along the hillside to keep from falling backwards, while Frosty struggled to follow her owner up the incline. But finally, after what seemed like forever, the pair made it to the top of the hill. Heather was thrilled to see the house that she had spotted earlier right in front of them. As she began to walk across the hot tar of the road, a sudden feeling of dizziness overcame the girl and she collapsed into darkness.

****

Heather hated the antiseptic smell of hospitals. It was an overpowering aroma that brought back memories of a hospital stay long ago. Visions of that experience flooded her head as she slowly opened her eyes. Blurry at first, they slowly focused on somebody sitting next to her. It was her mother.

"Mom?" asked Heather, in a weak voice.

"Yes, honey, it's me," softly answered Mrs. Richardson as she gently stroked Heather's hand.

"How long have I been asleep?"

"You've been in and out of it for a few days," replied a man's voice.

Looking past her mother, Heather could see her dad standing against the wall.

"Dad?"

"Yup, I'm here too," softly answered her father.

"Am I okay?"

"Oh, honey, of course you are!" said Mrs. Richardson, doing her best to reassure her child that everything would be all right. "You have a concussion. The doctor said you'll be fine but you have to take it easy for a few days."

"That's right," added Mr. Richardson. "No crazy horse trips for at least a week."

"Horse trips? What are you talking about? I don't remember going on a trip."

"You went on a three-day camping trip with Laura and a group of friends. Don't you remember?"

Heather stared at her father with a quizzical look.

Seeing the confused expression on his daughter's face, Mr. Richardson continued, "The doctor said that it might take a little while for you to remember everything that happened. Don't worry, Heather. It's normal to forget things after a head injury."

Heather's parents told their daughter about her adventure, being careful to leave out the part about her getting lost. Slowly, Heather began to remember details about her journey.

"I got lost, didn't I?" she finally asked. As if coming out of a fog, Heather started seeing things in her mind, things that had happened to her and Frosty.

The next day, while her parents were visiting, Heather was talking about her time in the woods of Vermont when she remembered...

"Something happened to Frosty. I remember she was hurt. I think she got bitten by a snake."

Heather paused as she suddenly realized she didn't know what had happened to her beloved mare.

"Mom?" she asked in a sudden panic, "what happened to Frosty? Is she okay? Did she, did she," Heather stumbled over the words, terrified of what might have happened.

"Frosty is going to be okay, Heather, you don't need to worry," answered her mom. Then she admitted, "It was pretty touch and go there for a while, when the two of you were first found. While you were taken to the hospital, Frosty was taken to a local veterinarian. We've talked to him, Dr. Curren, and he says that she is going to be fine."

"What happened Mom? Did she get bitten by a snake?"

"Yes she did. According to Dr. Curren, she was bitten by a timber rattlesnake. They tend to be very non-aggressive, but when they are cornered and feel threatened, they will strike."

As her mom talked, Heather remembered climbing the tree while Frosty searched for food below. Frosty must have found the snake resting amongst the rocks, tried to play with it and frightened the snake into biting.

"Dr. Curren was able to get the antivenin administered quickly."

"Antivenin?" asked Heather.

"Antivenin is what doctors use to treat snakebites," explained Heather's father. "It's the only treatment there is for a venomous snakebite and we were very lucky that Dr. Curren had enough to treat Frosty."

"Oh, now I know what it is. I have heard of that stuff before."

"Anyway," continued Heather's mom, "Frosty is too tough of a horse to give up. She fought and struggled and has slowly come around. She's eating now and the swelling is slowly going away. The plan is to ship her home to Dr. Reilly in a few days, once she's strong enough to travel."

"The woman who found you said it was the most amazing sight," interrupted Mr. Richardson, wanting to steer the topic away from the snakebite. "She said you were lying in the middle of the road with Frosty standing right next to you. That horse was just inches away from you but she didn't step on you once. Her head was down, right above your head and she wouldn't move. Even when the ambulance came to take you to the hospital, Frosty wouldn't move. It took a lot of encouragement, on the part of the vet and a few other people, to finally get Frosty to leave that spot."

"I think she was protecting you," observed Mrs. Richardson. "Nobody believes me; they all say she was just too sick to move. But I really believe Frosty knew you were hurt and wanted to protect you from harm."

Heather listened to her mother intently. In her heart, she knew that Frosty was watching over her. After all, hadn't they taken care of each other during their ordeal in the woods of Vermont?

"Mom?"

"Yes, dear?"

"Are you sure Frosty will be okay? I mean, if anything were to happen..."

"I promise, Heather. She'll be fine. The veterinarian wouldn't lie to us. He said that she would pull through. It will be a while before you can ride her again, but she'll be fine."

"You know," interrupted Mr. Richardson again, "when Laura called us and said that you were lost, we thought that…"

"Laura? Oh, my gosh," exclaimed Heather. "I forgot all about Laura. She's going to kill me when she finds out what happened." "No she isn't," said Mrs. Richardson. "She knows that you were found and that you are going to be okay. She was thrilled, trust me."

"Although she may never let you go on a trail ride with her again," joked Mr. Richardson, "but I promise you, she isn't angry."

"Where is she? Can I see her?" asked Heather.

"She went home, honey," answered Heather's mother. "Once she heard that you were found and everything was going to be okay, she decided to take Rusty home. She's called a couple of times to check on you. She said that she was going to take Blackjack to Dr. Reilly's today too."

"Blackjack? To Dr. Reilly's? What for?"

"Don't you remember, kiddo?" asked Mr. Richardson. "Dr. Reilly wanted to do further tests on him."

"Was that today? I don't remember," replied the girl.

"Well," answered Mr. Richardson, "I don't know when the appointment was originally scheduled for, but Laura said she was taking the horse today. I think she said they were going to take some chest x-rays. Hopefully when you get home, they'll have found the cause of all of Blackjack's problems. Now get some rest."

****

The next several days passed slowly as Heather regained her strength. She was released from the hospital quickly, but the doctor gave her strict orders to stay at home and rest. Quietly relaxing at home was torture for Heather, a person who loved to stay active. She felt fine, her head didn't hurt, and there were no more dizzy spells or headaches, so why couldn't she run around? More importantly, why couldn't she visit her two horses?

Meanwhile, Frosty, who was making steady improvement, had been moved to Dr. Reilly's barn. He had a beautiful, eight-stall barn right behind his house. With the exception of a couple of ponies that he kept for his children, the stalls were reserved for patients.

As Heather paced about her house, turning on the television, turning it off, reading a few pages of a book, then putting it down to get another book, or a drink, or a snack, or to pace again, she thought she would go crazy. She had to know what was happening to her horses. Finally, she picked up the phone and called Laura.

"Heather? Is that you? I'm so happy to hear from you!" exclaimed Laura when Heather called.

"Why didn't you call me Laura? I've been wondering what's going on with Blackjack and I thought you'd call."

"I'm sorry Heather. Dad told me not to call and bother you."

"Bother me? No, I want phone calls! I'm going nuts here, stuck in the house. I need to know what's going on with the horses."

"I wish I knew, Heather. When I dropped Blackjack off at Dr. Reilly's, he was in the middle of examining another horse. He also wanted to wait for Dr. Hutchinson to arrive since they'd been working the case together. His guess was that it would be at least an hour before they would get to Blackjack. I had a lot of errands to run for Dad so I had to leave. I called back the next morning but Dr. Reilly had left for a couple of days. I think he had some medical conference to attend. Anyway, the assistant who was left in charge wouldn't give me any information since I'm not the owner of the horse. All I know is that Blackjack is there, and that Frosty was supposed to arrive some time last night. I'm pretty sure that Dr. Reilly came back today. Maybe you could try calling his office?"

"Thanks Laura," replied a disappointed Heather. "I'll call his office."

Heather hung up and immediately called Dr. Reilly's practice.

"No, I'm sorry, the doctor is not in right now. He's on the road, making calls," explained Dr. Reilly's answering service.

"Can I leave a message for him?" asked Heather.

"Sure you can. He'll be checking in later today."

Heather, once again disappointed, left a brief message for Dr. Reilly, asking him to please call her as soon as possible.

It was after dinner when the phone finally rang.

"I'll get it! I'll get it!" screamed Heather as she lunged for the phone.

"Take it easy, young lady," scolded her father. "No running yet."

"Hello?" said Heather as she picked up the receiver.

"Heather? This is Dr. Reilly. I got your message. Sorry I didn't call earlier but I've been away for a few days and today I had several emergency calls and just couldn't spare the time to call."

This was it, thought Heather. Now she would know what was really wrong with Blackjack. She felt her stomach twist in knots and her heart began pounding faster and faster. Countless thoughts of 'what if it is this' or 'what if there is no cure' ran through her head at the same time. What would she do if it was bad news?

After a brief pause, she asked, "Do you know what's wrong with Blackjack?"

"Well," began the doctor, "Blackjack was very good. He didn't seem to mind the big, clunky x-ray machine at all. We took several x-rays..."

Why was he dragging it out? It must be bad news and he's trying to delay the inevitable. Whatever the reason, the suspense was killing her. Any longer, thought Heather, and she just might burst like a big balloon.

"...some from the chest area, others from the side. Blackjack was a perfect gentleman through the whole ordeal."

Please, thought Heather, tell me what's wrong!

"Anyway, the good news is that we found the cause of Blackjack's problems."

"You did?" asked Heather, momentarily relieved but then full of anxiety again as she waited for the diagnosis.

"Yes, we finally know what's at the root of everything."

"And?" queried Heather, unable to wait any longer.

"Your horse has an abscess at the base of his spine."

"An abscess? What's that? Is it an infection? Is it something that can be cured?"

"I haven't had a case like this in years. It is really very unusual."

"But what does it mean? Will Blackjack be okay?"

Trying to remember that not everyone shared his scientific curiosity and fascination with unusual cases, Dr. Reilly changed the tone of his talk to ease his young client's anxiety.

"Yes, Heather, he's going to be fine."

Feeling a huge weight lifted from her shoulders, Heather relaxed slightly.

"An abscess is an infection, right?" asked Heather, trying to figure out just what was wrong with Blackjack.

"Simply put, yes," replied Dr. Reilly. "An abscess is an inflamed or swollen area that is filled with pus, an infection. In Blackjack's case, the abscess was right next to his spine. The pressure against the spine caused all those bizarre symptoms that we saw. The strange backing up, the weakened hind limbs, the way the back fell away from the spine. All those things were caused by the abscess."

"Can he be cured?"

"I'm already working on that, Heather. I've got your horse on a new combination of medicines. He's on a combination of sulfamethoxazole and trimethoprim."

"Sulfa what?"

"Don't worry about the names," chuckled Dr. Reilly. "They are very long. All you need to know is that this drug combination is used to treat various bacterial infections, which is what I believe this abscess is. We'll know for sure next week when I do another blood test on Blackjack. In the meantime, he can go home."

"He can?" asked the girl, shocked at the simple conclusion to Blackjack's long ordeal. All it took was discovering the true source of all the problems so that the right medicine could be administered. "What about Frosty? Is she okay?"

"That little filly?" laughed Dr. Reilly. "I've never seen such a small horse eat so much food in my life! You better come get her too! My wife keeps coming out to the barn to feed her treats and your mare is starting to get fat."

"What about the snakebite?"

"The swelling is still visible, although nothing like what it apparently was when she was first bitten. I had a long talk with Dr. Curren, the vet who treated her in Vermont. From what he told me, we almost lost Frosty. The site of the bite on her nose is still sore, although the swelling around the nose is minimal. But there is still some slight swelling around the head and neck. Fortunately, Dr. Curren had some antivenin in his office as he occasionally gets snakebites in his practice. The swelling was severe but has slowly subsided with medication. I wanted to keep on eye on her for a few days to make sure the bite area did not become infected. Right now it looks fine so I'd say the chance of infection is low at this point. I think you can bring her home too, before my wife goes through a truckload of treats for that horse!"

****

"Heather? Heather?" hollered Mr. Richardson. "Heather? Telephone!"

Heather came charging out of her room. Dr. Reilly promised to call today with the results of Blackjack's blood test.

"Hello?" said an out-of-breath girl as she picked up the phone.

"Hey there, this is Dr. Reilly. Are you ready to celebrate?"

"What?"

"Celebrate! You know, have a good time! I'm sure you'll want to because Blackjack's test came back fine. He's cured!"

"Ya-hoo!" squealed Heather. "Thank you, thank you, thank you, Dr. Reilly! I'm so happy I could kiss you!"

"That's not necessary," laughed Dr. Reilly. "Just promise to let me know before you scream into the phone next time, all right?"

"Sure, I promise," said Heather.

Saying good-bye to her favorite veterinarian, she hung up the phone and asked her dad to drive her to the barn. Within half an hour, she was grooming Blackjack and giving him lots and lots of peppermints. Once he was sparkling clean, Heather left the stall and went to the tack room to retrieve more treats for Frosty. The gray mare had been eagerly anticipating her time with Heather and was hanging her head out of her stall, watching the action. Blackjack too, was now leaning his head out of his stall, hoping to grab another peppermint. As Heather walked out of the tack room, she saw two of the most beautiful Morgan Horses, with big, soft eyes, looking intently at her. With that, she suddenly realized Blackjack and Frosty would have the most beautiful foal!

AUTHOR'S NOTE

Although the story of *Frosty* is a work of fiction, all of the horses are based on animals that I have had the pleasure of knowing. Their personalities, likes and dislikes as well as their behaviors are all expressed within the pages of this book. Likewise, many of the human characters are based on people that I have known through the years. Blackjack's mysterious illness, with all of its bizarre symptoms, is also something that actually happened to one of my horses. Finally, many of the incidents, from the auction to the adventures in the woods are based on real events.